THE FIFTH
CORNER
OF THE ROOM

Israel Metter

THE FIFTH CORNER OF THE ROOM

Translated from the Russian by
Michael Duncan

Farrar Straus Giroux

NEW YORK

Translator's Introduction

Israel Metter was born in 1909 in Kharkov, where he studied mathematics in a technical institute. In 1929 he moved to Leningrad, where initially he taught mathematics and then during the early part of the war worked for Leningrad Radio. He was later evacuated to the Urals but returned to Leningrad, where he has lived ever since.

Metter started writing part-time in 1936: he wrote his first play in 1952 and for a time was scriptwriter for the well-known Soviet comic Arkady Raikin. Until the early 1960s his literary output had largely consisted of short stories.

The Fifth Corner of the Room (1964) is the later of Metter's two novels, the other being *Mukhtar*, the story of a police dog. Despite the intervening eventful quarter of a century, its pathos, its situations, and its Socratic dialogues retain their freshness and topicality. Looking back in sorrow and, more pertinently, with concern, Metter tries to hold a contemporary (i.e., as-of-that-time) mirror to himself and his contemporaries. His purpose is to use the Ariadne thread of memory to uncover "unlocated graves," to reexperience the past and, through understanding, gradually to come to terms with it. The strength of the book thus lies in its atmospherics: it avoids heroics – it looks for individual truths.

The Fifth Corner of the Room took twenty-five years to reach the public in its original full version. When Metter first took it to his Leningrad publishers in 1964, the friendly advice to him was that it was unpublishable as it stood and his best course of action was to pare it down to its personal love theme, removing the passages about Stalin and Stalinism, but in such a way that they could be integrally restored when the political climate permitted doing so. The result was his short story "Katya," less than two-thirds the length of the original, which first appeared in 1967 and subsequently in various collections. It was not till 1989 that, as it were, "Katya" and Stalin were rejoined in unholy wedlock as *The Fifth Corner of the Room*. And that same year, on its first appearance in its entirety in *Neva*, *The Fifth Corner of the Room* was chosen by that leading Leningrad literary journal as the best novel of the year.

Metter helps fill a literary gap: not what happened in the Stalin years or who caused it to happen, but how people felt about it at the time. His is a modest and partial response to Akhmatova's tragic cry:

> So much to do today:
> kill memory, kill pain,
> turn heart into a stone,
> and yet prepare to live again.*

This is a book about conscience and compassion and a sense of guilt, and about reexamining one's own past with their aid.

MICHAEL DUNCAN, 1991

---

* From "The Sentence", *Requiem* (part 7) by Anna Akhmatova, *Selected Poems* translated by Stanley Kunitz with Max Hayward, Harvill, 1989

THE FIFTH
CORNER
OF THE ROOM

Sasha Belyavsky, my best friend from distant childhood, died near Kiev in the first year of the war. But from well before his death our meetings had become so infrequent that when they did occur we each experienced a strange sensation: our long since past relationship imposed intimacy, yet there was no intimacy simply because it was all long since past.

We were bound together by childhood recollections that had frozen into immobility as if in an amateur snapshot. The sum total of what we remembered could be ticked off on the fingers of one hand: a country cottage or something of that sort, no longer real, near Kharkov; the hammock in which we used to swing; beetles in matchboxes; a thunderstorm accompanied by hail; cowboys and Indians. Kindly, reclusive childhood, fenced off from the world, from the malignant torrent of what is now called news from abroad – it conferred no right to adult friendship.

We grew up in very different families. Sasha's father, a baptized Jew, was a prominent Kharkov lawyer. In my poverty-stricken housing block on Rybnaya Street, our attitude toward people like him was mixed: respect tinged with contempt. Sasha's father embodied the dream of the pre-revolutionary Jew – higher education, purchased at the price of breaking with the faith – and this lay behind the ambivalent attitude toward him. In those far-off times, betrayal was still a cause for astonishment and, indeed, carried a higher reward than it does nowadays.

At the end of the twenties I left the Ukraine for Leningrad, and after that I saw Sasha only occasionally. He might come north on official business, or I might turn up at his parents' house in Kharkov. When we met, we would pick up at the point we had reached when we were children, and there was no way of progressing beyond it.

I knew that Sasha had graduated in philology.

He knew that I had never got to university to be able to graduate.

In the twenties it was easier for him than it was for me to step onto the educational ladder. Sasha had secured admission to his institute as a "category 3" – the son of an intellectual. There were five such social categories: workers; peasants; intellectuals; employees; the self-employed and others. I belonged to the last of them, the fifth. My father kept our family of six alive by working at home at any sort of job that came his way. That was when I first learned what a personal questionnaire meant and that it is utterly meaningless in terms of human life.

We lived in penury, but I bore the stigma of the question-naire on my forehead – the son of a self-employed tradesman. Forty years have gone by, and in all that time – an enormous proportion of an individual's life – though I chastised myself often for any number of sins, I never once succeeded in catching myself out in even a single venal one that might be described as specifically typical of the son of a self-employed tradesman.

I spent four successive years taking entrance exams to institutes, lugging my shameful documents along from one entrance board to another; and year after year I found my name was missing from the long lists of those granted admission.

I felt no rancour.

What I experienced was despair. Despair at luck not having been on my side. The revolution had laid down rules on which I did not seek to cast doubt. Those involved my being assigned to "category 5". That was my misfortune, or that was how I saw it then.

It was not till much later, in fact, that the other parts of the questionnaire became a torment in my life, and tormented me in an infinitely more acute way because they affected the fate of millions, and my despair was no longer purely personal.

I do not know how far back personal questionnaires go. Perhaps they originated with St Bartholomew's Night, when people used to chalk crosses on the doors of the Huguenots' houses.

I knew nothing of the circumstances of Sasha Belyavsky's death. A mutual friend told me that in that year of tears, 1941, Sasha had gone missing during our troops' retreat from Kiev. Tragic news at that time descended on people like an avalanche.

Some three years later a letter arrived from Sasha's father.

Sergey Pavlovich wrote that the search for his son had been fruitless. There were no eyewitnesses to his death, but one of the intelligence officers had notified Sergey Pavlovich that he had been the last to see Sasha. Military Interpreter Alexander Belyavsky, together with his infantry regiment, had found himself cut off and encircled by Germans. The regiment had tried to break out. Sasha had fought bravely alongside his comrades, but very few had succeeded in forcing a way through. Sasha had not been one of them.

And that, effectively, was all I learned of my friend, the friend of my remote, long-lost childhood.

However, as time passed, I would occasionally receive a letter from those Kharkov boys and girls. They were now old-age pensioners who, with plenty of time on their hands for reflection, were seeking to reassemble their lives. Scenes of my own threadbare past came back to me out of the gloom, lit up in the blaze of others' memories. They were an enigma to the bystander. I could not have recounted them.

There is a degree of mystification in the memory of an elderly person: I do not myself have the impression that my childhood is over forever and aye but that it happened once and must happen to me yet again. I buy the books on which I gorged myself in those far-off years – Mayne Reid, Fenimore Cooper, Louis Jacolliot – and, quite illogically, am convinced that they will still come in handy. I want to feel that my future childhood will be comfortable, that it will not catch me napping: everything essential must be to hand – exciting books, a football, a bicycle. I suffered enough for the lack of them in my first childhood. Or maybe it only *seems* now that I suffered so much?

[6]

What if it really does come? Shall I manage to behave as if ignorant of how it all ended? All my present-day experience will come flooding over me and I shall find myself well-nigh submerged in it. And the strange thing is that this experience will owe nothing to the achievements of world science and technology. In my future childhood I shall be quite happy, as before, with a magic carpet, with the *Nautilus* for a submarine, and with a simple rapier like the one used by d'Artagnan. Let them fend for themselves, all those atomic reactors and ballistic missiles. It wasn't they who enriched or impoverished my life.

But what am I to do with my lost illusions? What am I to do with those things in which I believed? And what am I to do with all that I wanted to say and do but left unsaid and undone? And not because I was short of time. I did have time to give the matter some thought. And I used to come to conclusions which frightened me.

*   *   *

Among the letters I received from those "boy" and "girl" pensioners, among their snapshots – against which my memory rebelled – I started to receive friendly letters from distant Samarkand.

Their author was Zinaida Borisovna Strueva.

However much I racked my memory, I simply could not remember that name. And yet she knew absolutely everything about my childhood and boyhood years. In each of her letters Zinaida Borisovna casually referred to names and events with such startling detail that I was astounded. Where on earth could she have learned of the doings of my courtyard with its fifth-category denizens. I myself had but the vaguest recollection of shaving off Monka Khavkin's hair, having purloined my father's shaving machine and persuaded Monka, my staircase neighbour, to give me the chance of mastering the barber's art. The machine clawed its way into Monka's fearful curls and hung there among them, a few centimetres away from his low forehead. My client's yells brought the entire population of our three-storey dwelling hurtling down into the yard. My father gave me an unmerciful beating. And here was Zinaida Borisovna writing to me about it.

In 1920 our living space was officially subjected to "multiple occupancy". Four women – workers at a tobacco factory – were assigned accommodation in our flat. Our biggest room, the dining room, was requisitioned for them. My present recollection is that it was about fifteen metres square. A two-tiered sideboard stood in the dining room: the women installed a piglet in its lower half. It was the calmest and quietest little pig I ever met in my life. In those turbulent, unceremonious times it conducted itself amiably and with dignity – a well-behaved, kind animal. And this too figured in Zinaida Borisovna's letters to me.

She wrote of how I fell in love with Nara Zolotukhina. Where does the name come from – Nara? And where are you now, Nara? Do you remember me clumsily pecking at your rosy cheek. We were standing in the corridor outside the improvised recreation room of No. 30 Seven-Year Technical School.

You had just finished reading aloud Bryusov's lines: "Bricklayer, bricklayer, in your apron so white, what are you building?" And the bricklayer replied: "A prison." I kissed your cheek, going quite rigid with adoration. We were both so naïve, Nara. It mattered not a scrap to us that at that moment the bricklayer was building a prison . . . a prison. We didn't know then, in 1923, that fifteen years later, the prison inmates would be our school friends: Nikolay Chop, Tosik Zunin and Misha Sinkov. They were in the same class as we were, Nara. Four of us came along to see you off: you were the fifth, and of the five only I remain on the earth because you too are no longer.

Who knows, maybe I owe my survival to being the son of a "self-employed tradesman"? Or to being a Jew? I have had it so often knocked into my head that fifth-category people are a particularly persistent lot. They survive regardless of fire and water. Dear Lord God, how many of them have perished in the fire. And how many are now being consumed in the slow fire of their own conscience!

My phantasmagoric courtyard at No. 28 Rybnaya Street. I don't remember how it used to look before the revolution. And this very same notion – revolution – kept intruding into our courtyard for long stretches at a time.

I read in textbooks about all the elements that went to make up my life. However, the net that historians use in their efforts to catch the product of actuality has much too wide a mesh. Such tiny particles as my courtyard, my life as a whole, escape through the mesh and I invariably prove to be small fry of no interest to history.

History finds it easy to explain the fate of an entire class, but to explain the life of an individual is beyond it. For that matter, heaven forbid that it should ever be obliged to do so.

For if the developmental laws governing a whole class were to be reimposed on the individual, he would collapse under the burden.

I would wish to be treated as a unique, unrepeatable person. And I am ready to perform the same service for the rest of mankind.

There is one method of making oneself unique, if only in one's own eyes: one has simply to recall one's youth. And it will seem a thing of wonder. When your own contemporaries are still living alongside you in the days of your youth, everyone has the impression of sharing the same fate. As time goes past, our fates twirl in and out and round about and start sputtering like a length of fuse-wire, and each of us then fizzles out or explodes in his own fashion.

There was a machine gun in our courtyard. Its muzzle faced the gateway. The gates were kept tightly shut and the sole main entrance through the archway was kept under twenty-four-hour guard by our own armed watch. Half a dozen men kept up a never-ending game of patience at a card table installed on the ground-floor landing.

My father was also a member of this defence watch – as we called it – in our courtyard. Father had a fatal passion for firearms. He collected revolvers, though he never fired them.

A strange aberration of memory occurs when one thinks about one's parents. To you they are always old people. My "old man" was then forty-plus. He could now have been my son. What year was this, Zinaida Borisovna? I am standing, jammed between my father's knees, in the synagogue. A loud, triumphant muttering enfolds me on all sides. Striped silk tallaisim cover the shoulders and backs of the congregation.

No faith is present in my soul. The noise, like a cloud of steam, rolls all over the courtyard. What they are saying is unintelligible and of no interest to me. I now can guess that they were talking about politics.

Many years later I paid visits to Catholic churches, Orthodox churches and mosques. How much more sanctity, fervour and grandeur were to be found there. I have in mind not their architecture but the religious atmosphere of the place of worship.

In my family they believed in God as a matter of daily routine. I was forced to say my prayers. But the compulsion exerted was the same as that to do my homework for school. On Rybnaya Street religion was a synonym for respectability and decorum.

At thirteen, when I came of age, I delivered the customary speech in the presence of guests. It had been written out for me in the two languages: in my native, living tongue – Russian – and in what for me was the dead language of Hebrew. The speech began with the words: "Dear parents and respected guests!" That is all I remember. I didn't even remember it once I had delivered it, for the reason that the dazzling Tanya Kamenskaya was among the guests sitting at the table. There was a ribbon floating in her chestnut hair. Now she is working as a librarian in Kharkov. We met in 1960. When I visited her at her flat there on Chernoglazovsky Street, Tanya managed to whisper to me in the doorway: "Please don't give my true age away to my husband."

She had no need to caution me: in my eyes, Tanya is an eternal thirteen years old. And when my future childhood catches up with me – after all it cannot vanish without trace,

[11]

it has to reappear — I shall present myself to her current husband and say to him: "If you have any decency, let me have my Tanya back. I give you a boy's word of honour that I will not so much as touch her."

We shall take each other by the arm and slowly descend the staircase. Slowly, because I have heart trouble and Tanya suffers from gout.

This is our courtyard.

We sit down on the bench.

Tanya adjusts the ribbon in her hair.

First of all we have our little count-off.

> *Eeny beeny race*
> *Quinter quanter chase*
> *Eeny beeny goad*
> *Quinter quanter TOAD!*

It always turns out with me ending up as TOAD.

"Wow, how beautiful you are," I shall say to her.

"Thank you for the compliment," Tanya will reply. "You didn't say so before."

"I was too shy."

"You used to tell me that my clothes looked so baggy on me."

"But surely you understood that I love you."

"It wasn't enough that I understood. You needed to say so."

"I love you."

"But why did you buy that dreadful Lidka Kolesnikova an ice cream?"

"I wanted to make you jealous."

"And then yesterday when we were playing at presenting each other with flowers you sent her an 'orchid'. Afterwards I had a look at the 'orchid' and it had written on it: 'I need to know when morning comes that I shall see you that same day.'"

"But that's Pushkin."

"You didn't send it from Pushkin but from yourself. I spent the whole night sobbing my heart out."

"Your Lidka is a twerp. I need her as much as a pain in the neck."

Tanya and I are sitting on a bench.

In three years Lenin will die.

In twenty years the Germans will be in Kharkov.

Excursions into the past of this sort are exhausting. You are faced with the blueprint of your life – for, after all, your life can't be simply a blank page – and you have no right to change a single line. Maybe I wouldn't try to delete anything but I would certainly make additions.

Nechkina, the historian, has a book, *14 December 1825*. In that slim volume she sets out, hour by hour, one day in Russian history. The mutinous regiments have been drawn up by their Decembrist officers on Senate Square. They are waiting for the signal to come out in open insurrection. Nicholas I paces furiously to and fro in the Winter Palace. The advantage lies with the Decembrists. They are waiting. Any moment now Prince Trubetskoy is due to appear. According to the terms of the conspiracy, he is to head the mutiny. On his command, the regiments will erupt into action. Trubetskoy is late. Trubetskoy fails to turn up. Nicholas succeeds in rallying the troops and in crushing the mutineers.

After reading Nechkina's book, the students at her lecture ask what if Trubetskoy had not been late? Supposing he had galloped up in the nick of time?

Academician Nechkina replies: History does not admit of these questions. You can't ask History the question: "What if . . ." What happens is what is due to happen, so far as that old spoilsport History is concerned. But don't I have the right to ask it so far as I am concerned?

Can it really be that within the bounds of my own minuscule life, everything that happened was bound to happen?

How many times did I want to act otherwise than I acted. So my personal Trubetskoy was also late in arriving? He was galloping toward the scene, somewhere over my shoulder; sometimes I seemed to hear his horse's exhausted snorting, but sometimes all that was visible was a trace of dust on the horizon. What a skunk you are, Your Excellency. And your mount is not a charger but a nag.

In 1920 our dwelling suffered a fire. At night-time the soot in the chimney caught light. Throughout the day people on the various floors had been baking hamentashen, triangular pasties with a topping of poppy seed. They were supposed to be prepared the day before the thanksgiving festival of Purim. The ancient chimney failed to withstand this ritual fervour – the fire spread upward and gutted three flats.

We sat in the courtyard on top of our bundles of household linen. Alongside us stood a basin filled with these silly pasties: in our excitement, we just gobbled them up, one after another.

[14]

I don't remember either my mother's keening or my father's state of confusion.

Only once in my life do I remember seeing my father confused and wholly at a loss. He was eighty-two when my brother and I brought him to the hospital in an ambulance. He lay on the stretcher in reception. Pulling aside the greatcoat with which my father was covered, the duty doctor had a quick look at his stomach grossly distended with dropsy, at his whitish lips plucking feverishly at small bubbles of air and then expelling them at the corner of his mouth. The doctor felt my father's pulse and squatted down on his heels beside the stretcher.

"A fine business, Doctor!" my father whispered.

"How old is he?" the doctor inquired.

I told him.

"Doctor," said my father slowly but distinctly, "in our country old people are entitled to respect – that's what I heard on the radio."

"Stay there, Granddad," said the doctor and went over to his desk.

"He needs to have the fluid pumped out of his stomach and to recuperate in an oxygen tent," the doctor said to us. He took his spectacles off his young, weary face, blew on them and began polishing them with the bottom of his gown. "Unfortunately, I can't register him. Your father's age . . ." He gestured with his hands. "Try going to the Head Doctor."

If I had done to the Head Doctor what I dreamed of doing during our conversation with him, I would still be serving time in prison.

Father died two days later, on the very evening up to which

[15]

the Head Doctor had agreed to keep him in a hopelessly over-crowded general ward.

They had not bothered to put a screen around his bunk for the benefit of the other patients, since an old man's suffering and death agony could be trusted not to spoil the mood of those around him.

The young nurse asked my brother and me to carry my father from the third-floor ward down to the hospital morgue in the basement.

We didn't know that we would have to carry him as he was, naked. It was easier for my brother – he took the head of the stretcher with his back to the body. But I had to confront my father's supine shamelessness all the way down those three flights of what seemed a never-ending staircase. I had never seen my father naked. I knew that even in death he would find it ignominious to be seen by his sons in such a state. With eyes screwed up, stumbling at each turn, I bore the swollen body downstairs. All the hurt and grief I had caused my father in life lay there spread out before me on that dirty tattered stretcher.

Forgive me, Father.

We buried you in the Jewish cemetery. Two old women in the empty rear room of the cemetery synagogue washed you and dressed you in the suit you used to wear on public holidays for as far back as I can remember. Dozing off and waking up in fits and starts, the old ladies sewed you, suit and all, into a burial sheet with a single long, unbroken thread. I know now what it was for: on arrival in that other world, which both of us in our different ways did not believe in, you tore out this thread with a single jerk and appeared before the Last Judgement shoeless but in your Sunday best. You had things to tell Jehovah. He hadn't, after all, made such a success of our human world as to have the right to summon people to appear before him in Judgement. And how did he propose to fill you with fear after all you had seen on earth? Was he proposing to summon a drunken Kharkov neighbourhood policeman and demand to see your residence permit? To charge you with eating matzo dunked in a Christian baby's blood? To summon the Hitlerites to appear before him? To hold a trial of the doctor-assassins for your benefit?

I am happy for you, Father, in that other world. There you don't need to be afraid of anyone or anything.

After the fire, we moved to Chernoglazovsky Street. The windows of our flat were on a level with the pavement and I swiftly learned to identify people by their feet.

Over the entrance to our house hung the modest sign:

PSYCHIATRIC CLINIC OF DRS ZHDANOV AND GUREVICH

The clinic was housed in a single-storey, yellow stucco wing of our building which on one side gave onto a garden. The patients, whom at that time people simply referred to as the madmen, lived in the clinic for long periods. The majority of them were inoffensive. Kindly and polite, they strolled in our yard and in the garden without any sort of supervision. They even used to wander into our basement flat to see us.

At first I kept my distance, but then I got used to them. In fact, they didn't seem all that mad to me and my companions. The interests and inclinations of adults are mostly alien to children; maybe for that reason I never noticed in our Chernoglazovsky madmen any striking deviation from the norm.

Vorobeichik was one who used to call in on our basement flat. Mother would treat him to a tea and saccharin. He would sit at the table, ceremoniously tucking his stubby little stockinged legs behind him under the chair. It seems he suffered from *folie de grandeur*, but I didn't notice it. Nor was his particular folly an impediment to those around him: he was so convinced of his greatness that it required no external confirmation. In that sense Vorobeichik's discreet mania compared favourably with the mania of normal people. Sometimes, affectionately stroking my hair, he would mumble speeches addressed to the members of the Constituent Assembly.

In all probability each epoch generates its own madmen: the most far-fetched delirium of a sick mind is, to some extent, a reflection of current reality. People go mad along contemporary lines.

Behind the one and only barred window in the Zhdanov and Gurevich clinic the white sail of Sonya's nightgown fluttered to and fro: in her mad frenzy she had constant nightmares of being raped by a squadron of Don Cossacks.

Patients from the Volga Basin also came our way. They had gone mad as a result of starvation. Their blackened, skeletal faces and heart-rendingly apathetic, dilated eyes frightened me. How could I have suspected then that in the winter of '41 in blockaded Leningrad I would have just the same sort of face.

A dreary young man wearing underclothes and a student's forage cap used to walk around our garden. His name was George Borman. In our childish way we at first teased him cruelly, but he managed to disarm us with his gentleness and his phenomenal knowledge of mathematics. Wee George, the natural son of the famous chocolate manufacturer, who had gone mad from unrequited love, would demonstrate problems of algebra to us on the sand in the garden with the point of a sharp stick.

Now, more than forty years later, I realize, after all I have seen and been party to, that our Chernoglazovsky madhouse was an amazingly old-fashioned one. Our madmen lived their own separate, intensive lives; they carefully cultivated their manias within themselves and did not attempt to impose them on the whole of mankind.

Don't be cross with me, Zinaida Borisovna. I had not forgotten you. And thank you for the two photos you sent me. I also received Sasha Belyavsky's youthful poems. Do you remember the elegant, guttural voice in which he used to read them?

We had got together in Tosik Zunin's flat. He had a swarm of small, snivelling sisters around him who were scrambling all over the floor. Tosik would pluck them off like kittens and redistribute them among the four corners of the room, but they would scramble under his legs again.

The head of the family, Ruvim Zunin, a First World War invalid, with acute trench rheumatism in his bones, was sitting on a stool in front of the gates and observing the life of the street. Mother was the family breadwinner. She conjured up ice cream from water and saccharin, and kvass from crusts of black bread. With this as her stock-in-trade, she went out at dawn to the "blagbaz", as Kharkov people used to call the well-known Blagoveshchensky Bazaar. Tosik, her eldest son,

[19]

who could hardly see, the pride of our No. 30 Labour School and a future young university professor, our unbelievably well-read young Tosik – the apologist for the French Revolution and an expert in political economy – carried his mother's ice cream along for her in a tub. His best friend, Misha Sinkov – the son of the Commissar for Postal Services of the Ukraine – would transport the laundry basket, full of bottles of kvass, on his back. On arrival at the bazaar stalls they unloaded their cargo. Tosik's mother timorously started trading. In order to attract custom, Misha opened his student lungs to their full extent and started singing in a voice of extraordinary beauty: "Once upon a time in the City of Kazan . . ."

Then he gave Tosik's mother an affectionate nod and said: "May all go well with you, Auntie. Tosik and I will be off . . ." Scuffing up the dust with their feet, lanky Misha led his half-blind friend off to his own house. In those days they were both fascinated by Marx's *Das Kapital*. Misha was the hungriest and most harum-scarum of us all. He lived with his father in an empty, virtually unfurnished, unprepossessing flat; the People's Commissar's wife had left him. Due to the extreme busyness of the father and the fecklessness of the son, they seldom saw one another but left each other notes and food in the kitchen. The notes were the briefest sort: "Needs some salt, Father" or "The spud's under the pillow."

The fact that our pal was the son of the People's Commissar did not concern us at all. In fact, we only learned of this long after we became friends. Our parents' professions were hardly of any interest to us. We loved them for what they were.

Where has this all disappeared to, Zinaida Borisovna? Just think: there were so many of us, decent, innocent, straightforward boys; we harmed no one, we couldn't have cared less about money, or how we dressed, or how we ate – why did we leave no trace of ourselves in the world? From what day, from what minute, did we start veering off course? For there must have been, for each of us, that one fatal moment!

I am sifting through my life as one might sift grains of barley, holding them in the palm of my hand and looking for the tares.

Are you, Zinaida Borisovna, familiar with the feeling of self-disgust? It comes out particularly strongly in the morning with the long day ahead of you in which to confront your own disgusting self. My generation has trouble with its ethical metabolism: we can no longer take in nourishment and we are virtually incapable of providing it – our memories fester inside us.

In days of old, the elderly had one advantage over the young: they had the impression of having lived more modest and meaningful lives. I have lost this feeling of superiority. And when the young people talk to me they give me to understand that they now resent my having eaten their portion. I didn't eat your portion, young man. And there's no point in strutting in front of me with your arms akimbo. Sasha Belyavsky and I combined to offer high school preparatory courses.

Our courses were pretty makeshift: Sasha was into his first year at the Philological Faculty, and I had just failed – for the first time – to get into the Medical Faculty. Together we managed to assemble a group of relatively untalented candidates for admission, and for a modest fee hauled them through the secondary school curriculum.

Science fell to me and Sasha took on the humanities. It

was then I made an important pedagogic discovery: if there's something you don't fully grasp, try teaching it. When I had to explain the rules of mathematics and the laws of science to my pupils, and solve problems and equations with them, I used to freeze into helplessness at the paucity of my knowledge. However, each time enlightenment dawned on me. It came about at the moment when I had to grapple with the problem myself. My naïve delight in solving it acquired magnetic force. My pupils were transformed into my accomplices. Could it be that the latter-day savage who hit on the secret of the wheel experienced the very same feeling?

I was recklessly unorthodox with my pupils, but they got into their educational institutions, astounding their examiners with the novelty of their methods of reasoning, while displaying almost sheer ignorance.

As for me, each autumn the admissions office of the Medical Institute would return my documents.

The path to the stars of higher education was barred to me. I needed to make a drastic adjustment in my "social status" entry. Father got me a job as assistant fitter in a privately run electrical workshop.

Now I became a "worker".

The workshop owner was a "NEPman" – that is, a small-scale private entrepreneur – who took on commissions from public-sector establishments. Two master electricians and their two assistants fulfilled these orders. And so, surplus value was being extracted from the four of us. In all probability it didn't amount to much, for the entire commercial workshop was crammed into one low-ceilinged, dimly lit porter's lodge. A long, untidy bench ran along one wall, and the corners of the room were cluttered up with broken chandeliers, sconces and table lamps. Whenever the orders dried up we set to repairing this bric-a-brac.

I seldom saw the boss. He would occasionally look in on us, pausing in the doorway. He cut a dressy figure, out of keeping with his years, in a proper engineer's peaked cap, even though he was no engineer. His sad bulbous eyes swept around the workshop. His corpulent face flowed down his stiff, snow-white collar like candle wax. He directed no instructions at us: he just stood there, his hands thrust into the pockets of his ample, tussore silk trousers.

I once went to his house: the boss sent me there with a message for his wife. Negligently half dressed, attractive and challengingly youthful, she was paring her calluses and lowering her small, strong feet into a basin. Casually reading through the note I brought, she said: "What a bore he is!"

I waited a moment but she added nothing.

The boss asked me: "What was she doing when you arrived?"

I was embarrassed to say she was washing her feet. "She was reading," I replied.

"Did she have any message for me?"

"She sent greetings," I answered. My imagination did not extend further than that.

"You're a good lad," the boss said. And gave me two and a half million roubles to buy myself a pastry with.

That autumn, after working for this odd "NEPman" for a year, I designated myself "worker" when filling out the Institute's admission questionnaire. I was summoned to attend the admissions board.

[23]

"Fitter's assistant," the board chairman read out in a loud, disdainful voice. He looked at me gloatingly. "Is that you – fitter's mate?"

"Yes," I whispered.

"Then allow me to address you a leading question. What is a Kurzschluss?"

I was silent. The foreman with whom I was working called a short circuit a short circuit. He never used the word "Kurzschluss". But he was a good foreman.

"Comrade members of the board, the picture is, I think, clear: we have a case of imposture. I move that we give this gentleman his documents back."

And I got them back once more.

Ever since those youthful days I have hated my documents. I have lived with the perpetual feeling that there is always something wrong in them. Something missing. And the missing bit turns out to be the most important.

Over the long years a whole multitude of certificates, credentials, passes and membership cards has accumulated. If one were to assemble it, systematize it and feed it to a computer, what the cybernetic machine of the future would cobble together from this data would not be me.

I have remained inside the machine, stupefied by its infinite impulses.

Historical events, and even facts, for that matter, devoid of emotional content, are hard to remember. Feelings take root in the memory more strongly than does logic.

The newspapers – I remember this distinctly – had only just started to come out with Stalin's name. We did not know who he was. I recall so sharply our feeling of puzzlement.

It was not because we were politically illiterate that we did not then know the name of Stalin. It was simply that his name did not exist alongside that of Lenin. Beside the latter's stood quite other names. A whole lot of them.

For us, I would have said, that period bore no individual's name, just the generalized one of "Soviet Power".

And before our eyes the period acquired the pseudonym – Stalin.

Perhaps because I had not received any formal education and no one had had an opportunity to impose on me from an early age a categorical view of life – maybe precisely for this reason – I had been free to make my own selection and reach my own judgements.

I had never been through any exams or vivas requiring me to proffer my thoughts about the world around me or my overall assessment of it. And since I was not obliged to produce them, my thoughts were my own, organically my own. I was under no compulsion to submit them in order to bring my marks up to the required level. I had the right to fail to understand and to make mistakes.

There were years when people like me were called philistines. If such a person were to express doubt about anything, he would have it contemptuously suggested to him that he was relying on gossip in trams, rumours from street queues. And yet it is the people, the men in the street, who stand in the trams and in the queues.

The philistine is in a difficult position. He always turns out to be wrong. Even when he is right. Either his judgement is unduly premature – that is, in advance of the government decree on the subject – or it comes too late in the day – that is, after the decree, by which time the subject is considered definitively exhausted.

Only posthumously does the philistine receive his due: history then redesignates him the man in the street.

The scale of falsification practised in the use of the term "the people" knows no bounds. From the thirties onward they started proclaiming who was of "the people" and who was to be expelled from "the people". In essence only one person – Stalin – bore the title "the people".

Disaster overtook Misha Sinkov. His father had left for the Commissariat and failed to return home. For three days Misha remained unconcerned – all sorts of things can happen at the office – but his father turned up on the fourth day.

Tosik Zunin was spending that night with Misha. The two of them sat in their underpants at the dining table on which lay a jumble of unwashed crockery. The kids were playing chess.

The door in the lobby clicked.

"Dad!" yelled Misha.

He rushed into the lobby to greet his father. There was a bunch of keys in his father's hands. Three men stood at his side.

"I'll put the samovar on," said Misha. "Shall I put my trousers on, Dad?"

"Put them on," said his father. "I'm under arrest."

He unlocked the drawers of his writing desk, handed over the keys, and sat down on a chair in the corner of the room as if he were a stranger to the flat.

[26]

The boys put their trousers on. While the brief search got under way, they sat silently on the couch. There were few possessions in the flat.

One of the police operatives, evidently the senior of the three, having rummaged about in the virtually empty drawers of the desk, scrutinized a piece of paper and held it out toward Sinkov, without letting it out of his hands.

"Why are you keeping secret documents elsewhere than in a safe?"

Sinkov glanced momentarily at the paper and answered: "What secret is that supposed to be? It's Lenin's Testament."

"We're not kids," the officer smiled. "You know what the matter is." He took a Nagan pistol out of the drawer. "And why didn't you hand in the firearm?"

"A presentation," said a terse and tired Sinkov.

The operative read the inscription on a silver plate soldered to the butt of the pistol. It proclaimed that the presentation firearm had been awarded to Sinkov by the Revolutionary Council of the Republic.

"You should have kept just the inscription plate in the house," said the operative.

He was still quite young, and had only just begun to savour the cloying, bittersweet taste of power over another human being. He was still apprehensive about making mistakes in his work, on the absurd assumption that in his work there could be such things as mistakes. He was still going to the trouble of figuring out what questions needed to be put to the man under arrest. He still considered himself to be defending Soviet Power against its enemies.

Ten years later, in 1936, this former operative, now with a

bar on his shoulder boards, was busy in his own office interrogating a young Kharkov University professor, Anatoly Zunin.

"Take a seat, Anatoly Ruvimovich," the ex-operative said when the two convoy guards hauled Tolya in. "Dear God, what a mess they've made of you!"

And he gave the guards a stern look. Two ignorant country boys, with twenty years of semi-starvation behind them, but now part of the convoy troops, well – even lavishly – fed, and dressed in clean clothes; two shamelessly misled soldiers persuaded by their superiors that the prison was bursting with spies and counter-revolutionary swine; two foreheads swelling with hatred toward the human race – for he who today was a human being might tomorrow end up as seditious prison garbage; two well-disciplined guards who knew the rules of the game. When their boss gave them his severe look, they looked properly downcast and intoned as one man: "Permission to leave?" And marched out of the office, knowing perfectly well that they might shortly be needed again.

The longish time it took the guards to proceed from his desk to the door was enough for the ex-operative: by the time they closed the door behind them he already knew what he needed to charge citizen Zunin with.

He did not treat the prisoners to any wide variety of approach. Even an investigator's powers of imagination have limits.

There was not a single country in the world atlas that did not have its spies among those investigated by him. The more people he sent to prison, the easier it was for him to imprison their successors, for each of the inmates had his family, his friends, and the very fact of their being family and friends

[28]

was grounds for a subsequent arrest. The monotony of the work was even beginning to get him down.

He was not particularly cruel or particularly softhearted. He did his job, day in, day out, competing with his fellow officers as best he could, so that, under the spur of this rivalry, he no longer bothered to consider whether the person standing, sitting or lying prone before him was genuinely guilty.

It was his work, his job . . . and that was to get the man to admit his guilt at the earliest possible moment because the section in which he, the ex-operative, was working still had a lot of people down in its books, who were also due to admit their guilt. And he became genuinely upset when one or other of these people pointlessly obstructed his work – pointlessly because sooner or later the work resumed its course, which meant that it should not have been obstructed in the first place.

As regards the ideas, toward the protection of which he devoted such incalculable effort, he no longer had occasion to think about them. Ideas were tantamount to theory, and his work was practical, and like all practical workers, he couldn't motivate himself each day with higher thoughts. Once upon a time, at the beginning of his period of service, he too had had a beautiful idea; it had gradually worn out and had become a little tight for everyday wear. He had made himself a uniform with which to replace it, added a raspberry-coloured peaked cap and some handsome leather boots, and proceeded on his way, the lighter for the substitution.

As regards his methods for extracting confessions, the ex-operative had become used to regarding them in the same way that a working man, a skilled worker, regards his set of tools. A carpenter knows when he needs a plane, when a hacksaw and when a mallet. The ex-operative also knew.

And just as an experienced carpenter knows how a wide variety of effort, depending on the type of wood, may be required to bring it up to condition, so too the ex-operative distinguished between the types of people who passed through his hands.

His mastery of the art lay in reducing them to one and the same thing. The art became a trade. He had already mastered the tricks of the trade necessary for inducing in himself the right state of mind. His anger and his apparent mercifulness were all tools of his trade. He only had two genuine, unfabricated feelings: contempt and fear. Contempt for those he bent and broke in his interrogations, and fear for his own fate.

He could hardly fail to despise those under arrest. The stupefaction and terror he inspired in them by all he did to them transformed them into non-persons, reduced them to the state where a man loses his individuality. He did have occasion to encounter tougher nuts, but he despised them too, simply for wasting their efforts: they were personally offensive to him, but he refrained from taking offence; they yelled or mumbled or with their last breath pronounced their dying words – and these were meaningless and artificial to him because such people had nothing to substantiate them with, no solid backup in the shape of the army, the secret police troops, the air force, the navy, the prisons and the camps, no government such as that which stood at his own back. These "tough" characters didn't even have any like-minded supporters worth speaking of: you could reduce their closest friends to such a jelly it made you sick to look at them.

Yet despite all this he experienced fear.

He was petrified by the thought that his trade might cease to be necessary. He was scared of retaliation, not from those at liberty walking the village and city streets (and he had weighty reasons for despising them too), but from those who worked alongside him and – especially – above him! The constant fear, nagging at his brain, that somewhere in the office one of his chums might be working more quickly and more efficiently than he tortured the ex-operative's mind and kept him in a perpetual scramble to improve yet further his methods and rate of work.

However, what he feared most was what was happening above him. That was where the main threat to him came from. It was impossible to anticipate it in advance. He witnessed officers who had entered the service at the same time as he had disappearing – always suddenly. Their disappearance was a gradual phenomenon, one stratum after another, and for good. First to go were those who remembered the reasons for which their predecessors had disappeared – and so it continued, one stratum after the other, always leaving behind just a hard core that never thinned out.

This constant threat hanging over him really poisoned his life. The fear only really left him at those times when he started interrogating someone under arrest, for then the ex-operative had to cauterize his own dread.

In the few hours he had off work, he lived a normal sort of life: he took his daughter to the children's theatre, the circus or the zoo, presented his wife with a flask of perfume on 8 March, played dominoes and football at the sanatoria to which he had holiday passes, flipped through the newspapers.

He had no close friends – who better than he to know the value of close friends!

From time to time he would meet his fellow officers at get-togethers on public holidays. Usually this occurred after the actual calendar date, because the first days of May and 7 November were the peak periods of their work. The job of posting men at intervals along the whole length of the route to be taken by the city's top brass to get to the parade, barring off courtyards which afforded a rear exit, clambering down into all the sewer outlets, sealing off the balconies, and then, in the evening, of ensuring that not a single person was present without a special pass in the front rows of the balconies, in the stalls or the boxes at the triumphal ceremony in the city theatre and at the subsequent concert – all these public holiday chores took up a lot of time and effort, generously remunerated by those selfsame half-starved citizens who never saw the parades, the triumphal ceremonies or the concerts.

His fellow officers celebrated the revolutionary anniversaries according to a calendar of their own which postdated the normally accepted dates by two days or so. They got together in suitably small numbers, with due regard to equivalence of rank and function. They bore an overall resemblance to one another – in the style and cut of their civvy suits, their soft, casual headgear and footwear, their socks and underclothes, their smutty stories and their prematurely aged, oafish wives.

They drank a lot and knew how to indulge. They never talked shop at table.

All of them were, once upon a time, working lads, country boys, failed students; many could have grown up to be decent citizens, but their corrupt, ignoble way of life, their monstrous work and fear, had had its attritional effect; they had ceased to be humans and had turned into butchers.

Sasha Belyavsky was the aristocrat among us. He moved from Rybnaya Street to Sumskaya Street, the town's main road. It was now called Karl Liebknecht Street, and Pavlovskaya Square had become Rosa Luxemburg Square. For us this was no mere change of name but a sign of the approaching flashes of the revolution.

Sasha had his own room in his parents' flat, with two carpets, one above the sofa and another covering the entire floor. There was a large ivory paperknife on his very own writing desk. Such knives are now a thing of the past.

It seemed the height of elegance when Sasha held across his knees a new, solid-looking book, printed on thick grey paper, its pages uncut, and, inserting his ivory paperknife between its pages, slit them, first horizontally and then vertically. The paper slivers showered down onto his newly ironed trousers. He brushed them off carefully onto his outstretched palm. When we went on to read the book, we had the idea that we were the very first to do so.

Sasha's parents knocked before entering his room. Sasha would bellow out: "Entrez!" or "Please".

He knew several languages, even Turkish. The only people he could speak Turkish to in Kharkov were the local Assyrians, the Aisors, as we called them. Thus his shoes always shone aggressively and he carried around with him a faint smell of the very best Funk boot polish.

He addressed his mother by her Christian name, Lyuba. It

bothered me. His life was so different from mine that I felt awkward when I visited his home.

Sergey Pavlovich went about indoors in a long woollen housecoat with twin tassels dangling down to his knees. He wore soft, embroidered slippers. A Great Dane the size of a pony ambled over the carpets, majestically prodding the doors aside with his paw. They addressed the dog, too, in English.

I had the impression that there was something phony about Sasha's household. They all seemed to me to be putting on airs: even the dog's pomposity was contrived. I could readily picture it – Rex was its name – reverting to mongrel in its time off and gobbling up the household slops in the kitchen.

Our group was not on the whole keen on going to Sasha's house and did so infrequently. We were treated politely and considerately, but there was something about the house that made us feel uneasy: perhaps the immaculate tidiness and cleanliness, or perhaps Sergey Pavlovich, whom we didn't understand and of whom we fought shy.

He adopted a studiously comic tone with us. He must have believed that irony was what we most appreciated. Our relations with Sasha, too, were on an abnormally ironical plane. Perhaps they both assumed that irony underlined their man-to-man friendship of equals.

At the start I was impressed by their ease of communication with one another, but I rapidly noticed that, despite the moderation with which their quarrels were conducted, when Sergey Pavlovich looked at his son, there would come into his eyes a sort of strange, pitiful pleading. I was not then to know how complicated were their relations with one another.

Outside his home Sergey Pavlovich led a very sociable,

indulgent life. Women went mad over him. But luck was never with him – he always came a cropper. Expert lawyer though he was, it was the trifles that gave him away. On his return in the evening, before opening the door of the flat he would scrutinize himself from head to toe and switch his well-fed, man-about-town expression to one of exhaustion and preoccupation. But this failed to save him. He still smelled of another's perfume, another's powder, of the pungent aroma of some city restaurant.

There was an awkward atmosphere in the Belyavskys' prosperous and elegant household. I had no idea why this should be so, but I didn't like going there.

Sasha and I used to arrange lessons with our students in my basement. They came to us in response to the stickers we put on fences.

"Two students," I fibbed, "offer tuition in all subjects for entry to higher educational establishments. Fees by agreement."

We didn't have such a tremendous number of them – half a dozen or so. From their point of view the attraction of our pedagogical facility was its cheapness; we charged a derisory sum.

Sasha looked the more imposing of the pair of us, and so it was he who conducted the preliminaries with our candidates' parents. He was nicely dressed and well brought up. I would only be produced when our pupils were no longer in a position to withdraw. I was got up in my middle brother's cast-offs, just as he had earlier gone about in those of my eldest brother.

Father had a wise formula, which he used to fend Mother off when she begged him to buy me some new clothes.

"How do you expect him to be recognized in new trousers?"
And it was true. People recognized me from a long way off.
Because of the picturesqueness of the rags I wore.

The only thing bought for me separately was my cheap
white cotton socks. Mother tried to object to their colour but
Father was adamant.

"The chief rabbi in Minsk wears white socks," he said.
"So how come our scarecrow ceases to be recognizable in
them?"

In our family it was Father who looked after the household.
I don't know why this was, but ever since I started to understand how things were run, Father had been the family manager. He even bought Mother's dresses for her. He made the
jam and salted the cucumbers away for the winter. He baked
the bread. He soldered and brazed the pots and pans; cleaned
and greased his revolvers.

At table no one dared occupy Father's place.

The last time Father hit me was when I was seventeen.

It's wrong to hit children. I've been through it. But I've
witnessed so much that is inexplicable in life that I have a
mortal dread of drawing conclusions. I came across families
where the children were brought up according to the latest
pedagogical methods. But when the time came, they turned
out to be scoundrels. I knew homes where parents who were
rotters turned out children of whom mankind could be proud.

The mystery, I think, will remain unsolved.

The conditions in which I grew up contributed very little
that was positive in the terms used by books about children's
pedagogy. Not because these books are a fraud. The one failing they have in common is that they do not take into account

the uniqueness of personality of whoever is doing the bringing up.

To bring up children by, say, Makarenko's method, one has to be Makarenko. The means of spiritually influencing someone cannot be divorced from the personality of its practitioner. That method must be part of him, an integral part. One cannot teach it. Nor is it possible simply to repeat what Makarenko did. The most one can do is to copy it. The copy will be more or less true to the original, but it will not be a living thing. One might be successful if each educationalist were able himself to personify Makarenko. But that is impossible.

Each and every mother brings up her child in her own personal way. With all the resources of her own inimitable individuality.

Your turn has come, Mama. People should know what a wonderful mother you were. When you died, I stopped being scared of receiving telegrams or phone calls at night. Your death laid to rest my fear for your wellbeing. Of your three sons, you always most loved whoever was the underdog at the time. And we always took it in turns to queue up for you because there was never a moment when one or other of us was not going through a bad time. When recalling their mothers, people cast back to their childhood. Not so I. I love you with a grown-up son's love. I remember your face when you used to open the door. No one in the world opened the door to me with such a happy expression. I used to tap at the window from the pavement. I had to wait a while at the door — you were on your way, stumbling along with the help of your stick. It is best that I do not recall the acrid smell of the damp in your flat. Be it accursed, that flat in which your concierge-neighbour called you a bloody Yid. You forbade us from intervening on your behalf. You were afraid for us. And we didn't intervene because we were afraid for you. And you had the goodness of heart to feed the concierge's son when he came out of prison. He had been sentenced for group violence, but you said to us that he was a good boy. And so it proved – he turned out to be a good boy. Your concierge-neighbour sobbed at your funeral. One can go quite mad, Mama, at the complexities of life. The longer I live, the more I become immersed in them. The only salvation, and it was this you showed me, is never to relinquish the capacity for marvelling at what is going on around you. As long as I retain that capacity I may hope to remain a human being. The most horrific thing about human vileness is not the vileness itself but the growing accustomed to it on the part of the beholders.

There's no one interested in listening to me now, Mama. For the women who used to listen with interest had others besides me. My close friends have worries of their own: they are themselves searching for someone who will comprehend their grief. But for you I was unique. Thank you for not seeking to "bring me up". You were simply there and that was enough, enough to last me a lifetime.

* * *

At the age of seventeen I went blind and deaf from love. Even now I find it difficult to realize that I have shaken it off. I was racked with this fever for fifteen years on end, right up to the '41 war. Time has obscured the outlines of this period of frenzy, but it did seem to me that I was ankle-deep in it.

It is impossible to recapture in one's memory the precise emotions of a deep, passionate love any more than of an explosion, or the feeling of flying in one's dreams, or a high temperature.

Whatever I did in those fifteen years I did either for her or against her. I lost the ability to perform neutral acts. Love became my profession.

I came to know Katya Golovanova because of one of our stickers. It gave Belyavsky's address, but Sasha was not in when he was supposed to be, and Katya suddenly turned up at my place on Chernoglazovsky Street.

As luck would have it, she chose the wrong time to come into our flat: we already had a visitor – Vorobeichik. He had spells of lunacy. It was then at its apogee. Usually calm and well behaved, he was nervously pacing to and fro in our dining room in his underpants, the strings of which were trailing along the floor.

It was growing dark in the basement and Katya did not immediately notice his pitiful appearance.

I had never seen such a beautiful girl.

Vorobeichik marched straight up to her, offered her his clammy, unwashed hand, and introduced himself, jerkily: "Rodzyanko."

"Katya Golovanova."

I subsided with horror on the sofa.

"Allow me in a brief, dispassionate dissertation," Vorobeichik launched into his best maniacal form of address, "to explain to you the spirit and direction of contemporary idealization. Pauperism, which occurred . . ."

[39]

"Solomon Nakhmanovich," I butted in, "the members of the Constituent Assembly request a break for prayers."

This was a sacrosanct phrase for him. He proceeded toward the eastern wall of our room and, covering his head with one hand, started to mumble the words of the prayer for the Sabbath.

I was now able to get up from the sofa and approach Katya. I was furious that she had witnessed my disgrace. When it turned out that she needed two student tutors as specified in the advertisement, I unceremoniously broke in: "That's a pack of lies."

She rummaged in the pocket of her jacket and produced a bit of paper.

"This is the address. I seem to have it right."

"The address is right," I said, "but the advertisement is all lies. I'm not a student."

"But you do give lessons?" Katya inquired politely.

"Yes, I do."

"I need a physics teacher. I've got behindhand with it." She held her hand out to me. "I am Katya. May I sit down?" She sat down, and I stood in front of her in my white socks. Vorobeichik was addressing his prayers to the east, alternating between a loud yell and a confidential whisper.

"Is he ill?" Katya asked quietly.

"A little bit," I replied.

"Don't worry," said Katya. "My father is a doctor. I'm used to it. Of course, Papa is a bacteriologist, but all sorts of doctors come to see us. Do you like medicine?"

"Not much."

"Please, don't turn me down," said Katya. "I'll be an attentive pupil. If you do refuse me, my mother will find some elderly cretin and I shall hate physics."

"Where are you studying?"

"At the Medical Institute. In the first year."

I had no right to accept her for tuition. Even as backward as she was in physics, the scope of her knowledge far exceeded mine. On learning the cause of my confusion, she stubbornly shook her head.

"Nonsense. In any case, you know more than I do. And then there are books, after all."

She left me her address.

The next day I visited her for the first time.

Katya lived in the Kharkov Medical Society building. On the way up to her flat I felt lost on the broad flight of the main staircase. The solid wall mirrors replicated my image: to my right and to my left a scraggy lop-eared young man in a much-patched student's blouse hanging down to his knees was impudently climbing up the marble steps. I was scared to look at him. But I was proud at what had brought him here. It was past working hours in the building. The vast, echoing corridors confused me. A penetrating, malodorous smell hit my nostrils: it was here that they prepared serum for the whole of the Ukraine. Now and then from behind the tall doors, like gates, came strange piercing cries and squeals. It was the monkeys and the guinea pigs complaining of their fate.

I finally came across a door with a brass plate:

PROFESSOR FYODOR IVANOVICH GOLOVANOV

Katya's mother greeted me coldly – there was no way I could have pleased her. Not merely because of the cast-offs I wore; I manifestly failed to measure up to the standards set by the wife of a Petersburg professor. Anna Gavrilovna, who was suffering from the indignity of Fyodor Ivanovich's transfer from the Army Medical Academy to head the Kharkov Sanitary-Bacteriological Institute, felt herself devalued in our city.

Nothing about it was to her liking: the feeble trickle of the Lopan instead of the mighty Neva, the Ukrainian accent, the bumpy cobbles instead of the smooth paving of the Nevsky Prospect, and the appalling mercantile architecture in place of Rastrelli, Rossi and Voronikhin. And now to add to it all – this young Jewish ragamuffin whom her wild-brained daughter had to bring into the house.

Anna Gavrilovna did not waste time on niceties. She indicated immediately that I was a nonentity. Under her icy gaze, it emerged that I knew neither how to stand upright nor how to sit or move about the room. I slurped my tea. At table I brandished my fork as might an assassin. My stresses were so appallingly wrong that I caused Anna Gavrilovna physical pain. It must be said to her credit that she made no attempt to disguise her revulsion. For quite a while she couldn't bring herself to utter my tongue-twisting name – Borya – but instead simply called me "young man".

The odd thing was that I did not take offence at her. Hostility expressed in so direct a form diverted me. The one who got annoyed was Katya. When Anna Gavrilovna really tore into me, Katya would shout: "Stop it! Stop it this minute!"

Our physics lessons progressed successfully. The Institute curriculum not infrequently had me at a loss, but together we overcame my ignorance. Katya and I immediately ran through the money which Anna Gavrilovna made into a painful ceremony of handing me for each lesson. I disliked receiving money for the joy of sharing Katya's company. I wanted to refuse the money, but Katya was furious.

"You're out of your mind! You worked for it! Why should you do it for free?"

I don't remember when I first told her I loved her. In the course of fifteen years I did it so often that all my declarations have fused into one.

It happened in the hilly part of the Technological Gardens – the entire city lay dark below us in the dusk – and when I uttered my words, Kharkov sprang into light at our feet just as if the intensity of my feeling had set fire to it. It also happened on Rosa Luxemburg Square, on Karl Liebknecht Street, in slummy, crooked alleyways, in gateways and archways, in desperately crowded trams and on the footboards of suburban trains. It took place in spring, summer, autumn and winter. In the sun, in the frost, and in the sludge. It happened the day she married Boleslav Tyshkevich, an OGPU senior lieutenant. And likewise the day she separated from him. And the moment I learned she had remarried. And again, when I married. And always when we were in bed together.

Of all human feelings, love must be the hardest to analyse. Analysed, minute particle by minute particle, it withers under scrutiny: dissected, it refuses to be put together again.

It is also difficult for me to talk of Katya because the facets of her character gave no idea of the miracle she represented to me. That does not mean I invented her in my mind. I wasn't even prejudiced in her favour: when people sought to point out her flaws to me, I did not deny them, I stubbornly insisted: "In any case, you don't know her."

I doubtless had in mind that the woman you love does not consist solely of the sides to her character. Between these facets are certain uninvestigated worlds visible only to the eye of the beloved.

I lived as though I were walking along an endless tunnel at the end of which there shone Katya. When this life became insupportable to me, I moved to Leningrad. The year was 1929 and I was twenty years old.

Mama packed into my suitcase two sheets, two changes of underwear, a pair of trousers and one freshly laundered student's blouse.

The day before my departure I went to see Katya. She was unaware that I was leaving. I kept back this piece of news till the very last second, without the slightest hope that it would in any way alter my fate. And indeed what was there to hope for? I just wanted to see the horror in Katya's eyes when she heard that I would be gone the next day.

We stepped out of her house and walked on, as always, with no goal in mind, not attending to where we were going.

. . . Thirty years later I arrived back in Kharkov with nothing particular to do. Usually meeting up with your past touches the heartstrings. The houses and courtyards seem smaller. Everything looks different from the way it used to.

In my case that did not happen.

On my stroll through the city I tried to conjure up old memories as I would perfumes. But the streets and houses would not talk to me. Even the smells and the sounds – those lasting props of the human memory – had lost their vigour.

I found myself walking round just another regional centre – my childhood's capital had disappeared. Possibly because my mind was then cluttered up by the debris of the present, and I couldn't emerge from under it to confront the past. The answer was that I had not become more adult, not grown up nor grown older – I had just become a different person. My boyhood had become detached from the set; it belonged to someone else. My impression is that many of today's old men experience the same feeling. Their life is made up of oddments. The trousers don't fit the jacket – they are different in colour and style.

Katya and I kept walking until late in the day and only when I took my leave, on her doorstep, did I say: "Tomorrow I'm going away to Leningrad."

"Why?" asked Katya.

"No particular reason."

"When will you be back?"

"Never."

"Don't talk rubbish," said Katya. "You can't go away."

"I shall do so nonetheless," I said.

"You won't dare leave me. I shall be lost without you."

"That's certainly not so," I said. "You'll be fine."

"And you pretending you loved me."

"Not a scrap."

"Not a scrap what?"

"Not a scrap pretending."

She started to cry.

"If you go away tomorrow, I shall do something terrible."

[45]

I was happy that she should be crying. My face probably showed this.

"You're a heartless pig," said Katya. "I don't have anyone closer to me than you."

I left the next day, after sending her a farewell telegram from the station. While the girl behind the counter counted the words, I stood so that she could not see my face.

"Is this right?" the girl inquired. "There are some repetitions. It could be shortened."

"There's no need," I said.

It was constantly happening to me: the telegraphists always felt a need to edit my telegrams to Katya: what I wrote tended to extinguish in them all their instincts for work.

I shall come to visit you in Samarkand without fail, dear Zinaida Borisovna, and thank you again for the invitation. I did receive Sergey Pavlovich's letter and wrote to him there and then. He tells me he has forwarded Sasha's front-line diaries to you. Please hold on to them till I come.

As regards your request, Zinaida Borisovna, I am sorry: I am unable to meet it. If it were essential for you, then, of course, I would write to all my childhood friends whom you listed in your last letter. But as far as I understand, you think it essential for me. And I don't see it that way.

It is late in the day for me to start building new friendships and renewing old ones. In both cases I am obliged to lay bare my soul once more and once again to assess whatever is disclosed to me. At my age one clings to friends who already know how one will act and what one will think. Disappointments make people more decrepit.

No, Zinaida Borisovna, an interrupted boyhood friendship is seldom reinvigorated. Even less frequently than a new one is put together. Perhaps because one always expects more from a former friendship than it is in a position to give.

Last year I made a trip to Rostov. The Institute's auditorium, in which I delivered my lecture, was half empty. The June heat had persuaded a number of outsiders to seek refuge in the cool of the building. My lecture was evidently of very little interest to them. The audience's mood communicated itself to me too. I hastily rounded off, on a feeble note. There were no questions.

However, as I made my way toward the exit, I saw that there was an old lady waiting for me in the doorway. When I drew level with her, she asked quietly: "Are you from Kharkov?"

A bit bemused by the heat and fatigue, I replied: "From Leningrad."

She looked at me and gave a confused, sad smile. I recognized the smile. The only person able to smile like that was Valya Snegiryova, on those occasions when I told her fibs. Nearly forty years ago I had lived with her for almost a whole year.

Now, standing in front of me in the doorway was a shapeless old woman carrying a string bag. And I realized that what she saw too was a worn-out old man, sweating with exhaustion. The feeling of guilt that I always felt when I was with her now transfixed me. I seized her hand and started mumbling whatever came to mind. I said to her that she hadn't changed in the least bit.

"There you go, apologizing for yourself again," Valya laughed.

We went out onto the sun-scorched boulevard. Even the blue sky looked jaded from its own efforts.

"Take me home for a cup of tea?" I asked her.

"I can't," said Valya. "My husband's taken the day off today."

Seeing my look of astonishment, she added timidly: "He can't bear to hear your name."

"Valya dear," I said. "Valya my sweet. Forty years have gone by."

"And so what," said Valya. "I have told him too much about you."

Dear Lord, and what there was to tell! At twenty-two I had married her on the rebound. She knew it. We had spent ten months together, and every single day of it was torture for her. With fanatical cruelty I had tormented her with my love for Katya. It somehow seemed to me more honest that way. Only far too late in the day did I notice what it cost her.

By now we were on a boulevard in Rostov, under the acacia trees. Subdued pensioners were whiling away their time on the benches next to us. They glanced indifferently in our direction – and we at them, each side unable to visualize what passions had once jostled for place inside the other. Along the alleys strolled the young people, of whom we had always thought, with casual contempt, that their fate was simpler and easier.

"How has life treated you?" I asked Valya.

"Life went on," Valya said. "It's too long a tale."

"Do you have children?"

"Two. They're both married. They also know about you."

"And they too can't bear to hear my name?"

"No. Not so," said Valya. "They would find it interesting to meet you." She smiled apologetically. "They can't picture their mother loving anyone other than their father."

"And if they saw me, would they be able to picture it?"

She nodded, not pausing to think.

"You are my infirmity," said Valya.

I had come across her at an evening party, when drunk, in the course of a visit to my parents in Kharkov, while on leave. Driven in on myself by my quarrels with Katya, I was trying to staunch the wound from which my lifeblood was issuing. I felt I had to do it there and then, in any way available. Early that morning I announced to my comrades that I was marrying Valya. Tosik Zunin took me to one side and said in a defensive tone: "In my opinion you're a swine."

"It takes a Talmudist to say so," I said. "She knows everything."

He rose on tiptoe, put his feeble arms around my shoulders and drew me to him.

"Why are you doing it?"

"I want to start a new life, Tosik. Do I have the right?"

"Wipe your face," said Tosik fastidiously. "You've got lipstick all over it."

On learning that I was preparing to get married, my mother invited Valya to supper. Father was away on a visit. My brothers had moved to Leningrad two years previously. We had the *pièce de résistance* for supper – braised tripe stuffed with flour and suet. We sat down three to table, an enormous one, Mother replenishing Valya's plate with the most appetizingly golden-brown bits.

"It came out all right, thank heaven," said my mother. "They don't always have it on sale at the bazaar." She glanced at me: "Why don't you go and fetch in a pail of water from the standpipe and the two of us can have a little talk."

I paused briefly in the kitchen and heard my mother saying affectionately to my bride-to-be: "Valya dear, listen to me, you oughtn't to marry him. I know my son – he will leave you."

"But surely he's not bad?" asked Valya.

"He's very good," said Mama. "But he's going through a tragedy. It's embarrassing for me to reveal his secrets . . ."

"I know," said Valya. "That's all in the past."

"Did he say so himself?"

"No, he didn't say so, but I feel . . ."

"And where is your mother?" Valya asked me on the boulevard in Rostov.

"She died."

In Leningrad I took lodgings in Sapyorny Alley, in the flat of a retired journalist from the St Petersburg *Stockmarket Bulletin*.

When letting the dimly lit servants' flat adjoining the kitchen, he first of all invited me into the lavatory and showed me how to release the water into the bowl.

"Please repeat that in my presence," said the proprietor.

His moustachioed wife warned me not to use the main stairs or the bathroom.

"That does not mean," she said, "that you should not take a bath."

It was as silent in the flat as in a cellar. Not a sound emerged from the owners' rooms. They both wore felt slippers and padded silently all over the flat, never failing to materialize from behind my back.

Whenever I turned on the light in the kitchen, they switched it off.

If I turned on the tap over the basin, they turned it off.

I might light the Primus stove. They would turn it down.

Before I went to sleep I would hear the scrape of the bolts, the rattle of the chains, and the clicking to of the locks. The owners shut themselves up for the night inside the flat and from me. It seemed to me they were not in the least bored at living in this utter isolation. Suspiciousness and mistrust of one's fellows pre-empt a lot of time and energy. Dogged by these feelings, one is kept permanently on the go. It's worse for a trustful person: for him solitude is unbearable.

For the first three months I saw nothing of Leningrad.

After parcelling out among a number of empty cigarette tins the small hoard of money I had brought with me from home, I feverishly set to preparing for the Institute entrance exams. I exchanged my entire pitiful hoard in the shops for ninety equal portions, giving me a rouble a day. Carefully wrapped up, they were an unbelievable temptation. To last the course I had set myself, I confined my daily promenades to the most boring circuits: utterly monotonous Basseinaya Street, the stumps of the side streets in the neighbourhood of my own Sapyorny Alley, and faceless Znamenskaya Street – that was all I permitted myself.

My documents were submitted to the Second Medical Institute. This time my scandalous social past did not play the decisive role. I fell down on my first paper on literature. Serafimovich's *Iron Torrent*, the theme I picked from the hat, was my undoing. I wrote that it was a boring, badly written novel which did not have a single memorable hero. Incited by my own freethinking, I had naïvely sunk my milk teeth into a work then considered a classic. The gamma I received for my critique prevented me from obtaining the minimum mark set for my category.

The frivolity of youth is something sacred – it engenders fearless deeds which one is subsequently told are axiomatic. And there really is an axiomatic inconsequentiality about them.

My money was coming to an end. My last cigarette tin contained eight one-rouble notes – eight days of life. On exchanging them in the cash booths for small coins and stacking them up in 50-kopeck piles, I doubled my capital.

The thought of returning home, to Kharkov, never even entered my head. I was in that state of physiological irrationality which reduces elderly men to a state of utter fury.

"What are you expecting?" the old man asks the young man.

The young man is at a loss for an answer because he expects nothing, and at the same time is expecting everything. Expecting to find a wallet left on the pavement; expecting that the door of his room will be flung open and in will come a breathless visitor to say: "We have a wonderful job to offer you. Please don't turn it down." The young man's expectations embrace the morning sun, the afternoon, the evening, and the night. And his own personal immortality.

On collecting my documents from the Institute I felt suddenly relieved. For four years running I had done everything I was capable of. That's enough, I said to myself. People contrive to exist without the benefit of higher education!

Now I had unlimited free time. At last I could look around St Isaac's Cathedral. I had often been told that one should start one's tour of inspection from the dome of St Isaac's. When I climbed up to the dome I did not think, as Rastignac did in Paris, that here at my feet was the city I had to conquer. There has to be, I thought, in this impersonal panorama, a modest niche for me too.

It can't fail to materialize!

"Let us have a chat," I said to him, excitably. "Don't you recognize me?"

"You're like someone," he replied, giving me a casual glance.

"Look closer."

"Your voice seems familiar to me," he said. "I've heard it somewhere already."

"But how about my face?"

"I can't remember it."

"Very well. To hell with it. I've probably changed a great deal. You see this scar on my cheekbone?"

"I see."

"You've also got one."

"It happens," he said.

"Where did you get it from? Hold on. I'll tell you. When you were four years old, you got laryngitis from stuffing yourself with ice cream in Yarotsky's shop on Rybnaya Street. Your father . . ."

"You knew my parents?" he broke in swiftly.

"I was their son."

"Tell me another one," he said. "I never had a third brother."

"Nor did I."

"Well, in fact . . ." he said impatiently. "Is there something you want from me?"

"There is . . ."

"What, precisely?"

"I want you to talk to me. I need to know who you are. I know everything about you, but I don't understand it all. I can be useful to you, after all."

"If you have advice in mind, I have enough of that already."

"You should realize I know how it will all end."

"In what sense?" he said casually.

"I know what you'll have to go through. You'll get upset if I tell you."

He smiled.

"All old men, for some reason, like frightening young men. You're about to tell me that I had it easy and that in your time things were different."

"My time is your time," I said to him in a voice of desperation. "Try to believe in a miracle: I am you!"

He looked at me attentively for the first time.

"How old are you?"

"Sixty."

"Not bad," he said. "That means I have another forty years ahead of me."

"You idiot!" I shouted. "They will be gone before you even turn around to have a look."

"That really is old hat," he said. "Even at sixty I wouldn't want to be guilty of such sentiments."

"You're right," I said. "Forgive me. It's terrible that we can't come to an understanding. Aren't you at all worried about my future?"

"May I put a question to you?"

I nodded.

"Are you married?"

"Yes."

"To Katya?"

"No."

He lost all interest in me.

"Is that all?" I said in astonishment. "After all we have forty years between us. Ask something else."

I saw quite distinctly that I was now boring him. I knew that he was rushing off to the Vladimir Club, where, for the first time in his life he was due to stake his last three roubles on the "red" at the roulette table.

"Shall we be flying to the moon?" he asked out of politeness.

"We shall . . . But before that there'll be war!"

Dear Lord, how flat it sounded when I said it.

"And we shall win," he said with assurance.

I found it disgusting to look at him. A snivelling youth, barely out of secondary school, a loafer unable to earn his daily bread, a sexual psychopath indifferent to all around him except his girlfriend, who despised him . . .

"On your way," I said to him. "On your way, you Kharkov ragamuffin. You'll live to shed tears of blood!"

And he left.

As they write in the newspapers nowadays, no substantive conversation took place between us.

*

I went without proper meals, existing off the contents of the food parcels sent me by my parents. My advertisements had long been on public display among others of their kind from equally starving would-be tutors.

My last three roubles I blew in the Vladimir Club, a gaming house for spendthrifts and profiteers. It happened with such magical speed that I didn't have time to taste the bitterness of the loss.

The croupier called out: "Faites vos jeux," and I, from behind a number of anonymous shapes, furtively slipped my three one-rouble notes to the end of the table. Through the total silence, redolent of perfume, sweat and anxiety, I heard some sort of rustle – and it was all over.

I did not even succeed in making out the gamblers' faces: a dense barrier of heads, necks and backs hid the table from my eyes, and every so often a wave of excitement rippled along the barrier.

On tiptoe I examined by way of a final gesture the croupier's ivory parting, gleaming through the tobacco haze. He sat on a dais. It was semi-dark in the big room but around this sharpster's head clung the electric aureole of a saint.

The roulette room was located at the far end of the club. On my way to the exit I walked through a number of rooms, equally dim and stuffy. Only the long, baize-covered tables were lit up. Here the professional gambling took place – baccarat and chemin de fer. Men and women, complete strangers to one another, sat in chairs alongside the table. They played in silence like ghosts. The feeling of unreality at what was happening there has stayed with me up to this day. I seemed unreal to myself that evening.

I had no money left for the tram. I walked up Nevsky Prospect from the corner with Vladimirsky Street all the way to the Moscow Station. To me, having just emerged from the gambling house, Nevsky looked different as if it were bathed in a mist of passion and vice.

Smart cab drivers, perched on top of their vehicles, awaited clients at the doors of the restaurants. Their glossy steeds, covered with blue sweat blankets, twitched nervously. The prostitutes, whom I had hardly been aware of before, started talking at me as if sensing that a gambler might require their services. They strode past at the street corners and in front of the brightly lit shop windows, dolled up in furs, feathers and war paint like Indian warriors. The closer I got to the Moscow Railway Station, the more bedraggled and impudent their appearance. At Pushkin Street, not far from the public baths, the tarts were ageing whores, with red faces, who stank a mile off of vodka, tobacco, and saunas.

That evening, the whole of the Nevsky seemed to me to be absorbed in losing at cards, parading itself for sale or inspecting itself for purchase.

The next morning I went along to the Labour Exchange.

I had visited it more than once before, but had come away in despair: the crowd at its entrance spilled over onto the street. The reception hall was divided up into compartments where the employees were seated at their desks. There was a buzz of muted conversation among the unemployed standing in line. These queues, which thickened out toward their tails, ended in a confused huddle on Kronverk Street.

That morning I was full of determination. First of all, I needed to get my name down on the register at the little window. This I had never succeeded in doing. I didn't know who I was. Each little window dealt with a specific profession. I considered myself a professional worker but all I carried with me was just the one bit of paper certifying that I really had been born and continued to exist.

That day in the hall I had mentally to revise my qualifications in their entirety. It was my good fortune that a job specification had just arrived from the Nikolsky Market: a pharmaceutical depot located at the Market needed manual workers.

For the best part of a month I manhandled sacks at the depot – and these I had to lug from the store up along a slippery plank propped against a trapdoor and onto the second floor. I had no idea what was inside the sacks, but they were very large and reeked of drugs.

With a day's stench of them in my nostrils, I couldn't eat. But my enforced fast so weakened me that I couldn't heave the sacks up the plank. The last two or three days were hell for me.

The sheer weight was proving too much.

I started coming to a dead halt.

There were green and red stars in my eyes.

"What, lost in thought, eh, brainbox!" the storeman would shout up at me from below.

And then I would call Katya to mind.

She would surface in front of me in the trapdoor opening.

"You can do anything," she said. "I'm waiting for you up at the top."

I would walk in her direction, my legs crumpling under me. The religion of my love for her kept coming to my rescue.

"You can do anything," her voice insisted when I was no longer capable of a thing.

"You're not afraid of anything," Katya would say if I was mortally scared. "I love you" – her whisper would come to me at the instant when solitude was closing in over my head.

Why do we tend to recall a difficult youth in more affectionate and vivid terms than a carefree one? Perhaps because we had the strength of mind not to despair?

Minor subterfuge helped me to get on my feet. My brother took pity on me and gave me his certificate to present to the Labour Exchange. The two of us had the same "inishalls", as the registration clerk at the Exchange chose to say. The certificate stated that the bearer was a mathematics teacher at a crash course for training cooks. The course had ceased to exist, giving me the right to get my name down on the register.

Amazing how my entire life depended on such a minor detail!

What is so hard to retrace in one's memory of the distant past is not the facts, which need no prompting, but one's thoughts, one's attitude toward one's surroundings at that time; and it requires effort to recapture them accurately.

The most difficult thing of all in visualizing one's youth is to remember to wipe your feet before entering, to present yourself stripped naked of your present experience and present thoughts.

When, after much painful exertion, I manage to impose the effort on myself, my eyes light on a world in which there is no law of gravity. That other naked young man on that other planet went about as effortlessly as a demigod: the least movement sufficed to launch him into space. He skipped along on carefree legs. He was able, in the winking of an eye, without a moment's second thought, to make the decisions on which his future fate depended.

If there was anything he should find unintelligible, he dismissed it as nonexistent.

The infallibility of his judgement opened up for him a wide swathe as smooth as a runway.

I do not know to what extent this youth was typical of his time. And does it in fact really matter?

What did I then think about? How did I live?

Empathy with everything that was happening in the world. Distances did not exist for me in my youth. Everything that moved me had to be happening next door.

Next door in England the miners were on strike. Granada was spread out in the next room. Around the corner they were building Magnitogorsk and the Dnieper Power Station. Beneath my windows Mayakovsky and Babel, Pasternak and Bagritsky, were to be found strolling by.

In my youth there were no games. For us football and hockey had not yet been invented. They hadn't even laid on chess. When we met one another, we did not play at anything. We talked.

I had a voice in the course of events, in determining people's fate. Whatever happened around me depended on me too. World problems impatiently awaited my contribution. I was disposed to be generous – I had the entire globe as my arena.

My judgements had one make-believe foundation: people

want justice and hate oppression. Human vileness for me was an attribute of class.

I believed in what I said. And I said what I believed.

* * *

This time around, the professional workers' branch of the Labour Exchange assigned me as teacher to a technical training school. The school was housed in the Alexander Nevsky Monastery, in the building where the monks used to live.

Twice a day I had to walk the length of the famous cemetery, past the graves.

It caused me no anxiety.

Everything that concerned the old way of life and death seemed to me safely immured in textbooks. I lived in passionate, insuppressible curiosity about the morrow: the evening's events tended to be overtaken by those of the next morning. I still had not realized that a person without a past is like an insect with a one-day life cycle.

The Timiryazev Technical Training School turned out auto mechanics. The "Tech-tiddlers", as they used to be called, were from such different educational backgrounds that I had to ladle out my mathematics in sufficiently minute portions for them to be swallowed at a gulp.

The then current term for this method was "pro-paediatric". I felt too embarrassed to ask what the word meant and I still have not managed to ascertain its real significance. However, the essence of it was that an idea requiring scientific proof should be put across by circuslike methods.

For my geometry lesson I would appear before my "tiddlers", laden down with sections of plywood. These sections were then hung up on the wall in front of the blackboard, and like a conjuror, I would give a tug at the thread attached to them, with the result that the large plywood square lying on the hypotenuse of a right-angled triangle would fall apart into two smaller ones, attaching themselves to the opposite and adjacent sides of the triangle.

I became extremely skilled at doing this, though I did initially have the impression that there was an old Greek by the name of Pythagoras moaning silently at the back of the class.

How often, using the same "pro-paediatric" method, though much later on, did people try to inculcate in me truths infinitely more dubious than Pythagoras' immortal theory.

I did not stay long at the technical training school. I doubt whether any of my pupils has remembered my name. I did not teach them anything worthwhile.

It was in fact they, those homeless, restless young boys and girls, who taught me something: the need to be understood. When you go into a classroom to be confronted by forty kids, sitting at their desks, famished with ignorance, their little birdlike mouths gaping in your direction, you cannot permit yourself the ignoble luxury of speaking above their heads.

I received my first wages at the school – three hundred roubles. It was ten times more than I had hitherto run through in an entire month.

The old chauffeur who gave the kids in my classes driving lessons was next in line to receive his money. Seeing my nonplussed look as I started stuffing the money away in my pockets, the old chap said: "I'd appreciate a word with you, Comrade Teacher."

[62]

I waited for him at the entrance, assuming that he wanted to talk about our pupils: we had helped one another on occasion.

The boys loved the old chap: he had driven some of the earliest motorcars in Russia, had been a racing driver and also a chauffeur to one of the Grand Dukes. He had fallen out with the Duke, who once, after too much to drink with the Tsar in the Winter Palace, had tried to sit at the wheel. Stepan Ivanovich had no truck with that kind of escapade. First he tried polite dissuasion on the Duke and, when that failed, he lost his patience and let fly at him in the ripest language. The Duke was very upset, they both lost their tempers, and an irreparable breach was established between them.

"And we lost our respect for one another," Stepan Ivanovich explained to me. "So I handed in my notice. And it was then that the February Revolution came along."

"And was that the last time you saw him?" the lads asked.

"So help me, that was the last time."

From looking at Stepan Ivanovich, I had no doubt about the truth of his story. He was a self-reliant sort of chap. As regards the Grand Duke, who knows – there must be all kinds of Grand Duke. One of them was the author of the song "The Poor Lad Died in a Military Hospital" – not a typical achievement for the House of Romanov.

I waited until Stepan arrived at the entrance and we walked together past the cathedral and along to the Staro-Nevsky district.

"Let's have a beer," the old man proposed.

We popped into the Cultural Beer Bar, as it was then called. The old man ordered two beers. Here, it came with salted peas and heavily salted crackers.

I did not care for beer, but out of respect for Stepan I sipped at it, slowly and deliberately.

"What a load of rubbish," said the old chap. "Why a 'cultural' bar? Does it mean if I get sozzled, I'm not a pig? No! D'you know who thought it up? Your country peasant did. He landed in the city and couldn't set about shuffling off his ignorance fast enough. So he started giving everything new names – 'cultural' hairdressers, 'cultural' lavatories, etc. He paired a decent word up with a lot of shit and was happy to have done so."

I replied something to the effect that the urge for self-education was a positive phenomenon. Stepan nodded politely but listened without interest. He interrupted me halfway through a sentence.

"Before you get yourself a wife, you need to get yourself a proper suit."

I stole a glance at my ageing student's blouse.

"If you like," said Stepan, "we can pay a visit to a tailor I know. He used to turn out men's tail coats. But now he works in a special governmental workshop. He caters to hunchbacks and higher-ups."

It was difficult to gain access to the establishment in question, but the old man helped me. I found myself armed with a chit, and the famous tailor was given advance notice of my existence. As I understood, Stepan had been friends with him for a long time. Which category I came under – hunchback or high-up – didn't particularly bother me. I remembered this tailor particularly, not because he equipped me with my first suit, but because of the personal impression he made on me.

When I entered the workshop Yakov Zakharovich was drinking tea.

A little further on, squatting on top of broad tables, their legs tucked under them, sat the trouser makers. Yakov Zakharovich was enjoying his tea, with a slice of lemon, at a separate, small table. A grey-haired, elegant figure with a neat white handkerchief peeping out of the top pocket of his beautifully cut velvet jacket, he rose to greet me, casually accepted the chit I held out, and dropped it onto the table without looking at it.

"With your permission, I will finish my tea," said Yakov Zakharovich.

He handed me a fashion journal.

"Have a look through it," said the tailor. "I will be most distressed if you choose anything from it."

At the age of twenty I had very little idea about fashion, and I flipped through it listlessly. What most attracted me was the possibility of avoiding choosing anything.

"Let us make a start," said Yakov Zakharovich, rising to his feet and flexing his long, thin fingers like a pianist before a keyboard. "Please walk toward the window and then in my direction."

I walked across to the window like someone on his way to the scaffold.

"Please relax," Yakov Zakharovich requested gently.

I proceeded toward him as he had instructed.

He placed his soft hands on my shoulders and with what seemed a barely perceptible pressure of his fingers conjured up the melody, as it were, of my future jacket, audible only to him, from my figure.

[65]

This was no hocus-pocus on his part. I had an artist in front of me. For those few minutes I was his creation in the making.

"Lidiya Nikolaevna," Yakov Zakharovich called to someone in the background, "please take the measurements down."

And with the faintest touch of his fingers over my body, he dictated in a quiet voice, not all at once, but between pauses during which his face registered a whole range of thoughts and emotions.

"Right shoulder – eighteen centimetres," he instructed. "Left shoulder – seventeen. Right shoulder blade half a centimetre lower than left."

Probably noticing my astonishment, he said: "Don't worry, every individual is different. And only a real expert can solve the riddle."

I have never in my life had a better suit than the one Yakov Zakharovich made for me. Even twelve years later, in the blockade year of 1941, I got a fantastic price – three kilos of snipe – for it at the Kuznechny Market.

Even so, it wasn't the suit that carved Yakov Zakharovich a lasting niche in my soul: it was the fact of his being the first to treat me as a person in my own special right, with my own special measurements.

The moment I found my feet the heavens fell in on me. Professor Golovanov and family returned to Leningrad from Kharkov.

Katya and I had not seen one another for more than a year. During that period I had received two letters, from which one could establish what she was feeling but not what she was doing. I had myself sent her two similar letters, bearing no relation to my life at that time.

I learned from what she wrote that she had split up with her OGPN operative, Tyshkevich, and had married an actor, Astakhov. Katya referred to this en passant, as if it were something self-evident.

She had fallen in with Boleslav Tyshkevich earlier, when I was still living in Kharkov.

He was some ten years older than we were, an enigmatic blond, with the impassive, well-bred face of an intelligent ascetic. Yet even while looking at him, I was inventing an appearance for him. A man whose profession was the daily fight against counterrevolution in no way fitted into any set pattern of external appearance. Even as I watched, his face dissolved into the lineaments of legend.

This face was what Katya fired at with a revolver.

On one of our walks, caught in a downpour, we had knocked at his door – he lived near the University Garden. Seeing that we were soaked through, Tyshkevich gave us clothing of his to wear. I received a raincoat and Katya his uniform trousers, jacket and cavalry boots. Both of us, Tyshkevich and I, looked at her lost in admiration.

She stomped through the room in boots far too big for her. The revolver was lying on a stool beside the sofa and the bullets lay in a heap nearby. Katya picked up the gun and, screwing up her eyes, aimed it at Tyshkevich.

"Scared?"

"Absolutely not. It's not loaded."

"But people say you shouldn't play about with firearms," said Katya.

"They say," answered Tyshkevich.

"And aren't you the weeniest bit afraid?"

He shrugged his shoulders, staring at her as if bewitched.

"Very well," said Katya, "I'll simply give the order, as in the books."

And she ordered: "At the enemies of the revolution – fire!" The room shattered at the sound of the shot. Tyshkevich fell to the floor. But he raised himself on his knees immediately and, supporting his bloodstained face in his hands, said: "Remember: I was cleaning the revolver. Put it beside me."

The ambulanceman came for him within ten minutes. The bullet had gone through his cheek without hitting a bone. The account given in the official report was to the effect that the wounding had occurred as a result of careless handling of the firearm on the part of its owner.

That shot determined the shape of their relationship. Katya looked after Tyshkevich while he was ill. She did so with such a feeling of self-guilt and admiration for his bravery that nothing more remained for her than to reward Boleslav with the most precious thing in her possession – herself.

Their marriage reduced Katya's parents to a state of horror. A Chekist in the house of a Petersburg professor, taking tea with them . . . ! The thought was more than Anna Gavrilovna could bear. She would have put a curse on her daughter, had she not known that Katya would not give a rap for it. Fyodor Ivanovich was likewise horrified – he followed his wife's lead in everything except his work, but the fight against disease was in fact of more profound concern to him than what went on around the tea table.

"I demand that you speak to her, Fyodor," Anna Gavrilovna started nagging at him.

"Certainly," he said.

"Katya dear" – he caught his daughter in the corridor of the Medical Institute – "we need to have a talk . . ."

Rising on tiptoe, she gave him a kiss on the cheek. "I was at your lecture. You were so splendid, Papa!"

"Did you really like it?"

"Tremendously. And all the other girls did too!"

Bringing to mind his weighty parental responsibility, Fyodor Ivanovich mumbled: "The fact of the matter is . . ."

"The fact of the matter is that Mama asked you to talk to me. She can't abide Tyshkevich. And I don't want what she doesn't want. I can stop visiting the house. Then you'll come and pay me secret visits, won't you, Papa?"

Now totally confused, he answered: "Very well."

On her return home, Anna Gavrilovna asked: "Did you speak to her?"

"Yes, I did."

"And how did she react?"

"She promised to think it over."

The marriage was doomed from the very start. It was founded on Katya's state of ecstasy. When the ecstasy lost its lustre and was worn away at the joints by the daily grind of keeping each other company, it swiftly emerged that Tyshkevich was a very limited person. His meaningful silence was explained by the fact that he had nothing to say.

All of us had one reliable criterion for judging someone else – poetry. None of us, apart from Sasha Belyavsky, wrote verses, but to be passionately fond of poetry seemed to us an indispensable requisite.

When we bawled out things from Blok and Gumilyov, Mayakovsky and Pasternak, Tyshkevich's face went rigid. He looked at us with politely dead eyes. That, Katya could not forgive him.

I quite realize how frivolous it was to judge people by this poetry criterion. But what am I to do about it if even now I continue to have the idea that someone who melts with enthusiasm at the lines:

On the cry: "There's mutiny brewing,"
He would wrench free the gun at his waist,
With the gold dust thinly cascading
From his cuffs trimmed with fine Flemish lace.*

– that such a person's reactions will run on much the same lines as mine. It is a sort of password for admittance back into my generation.

I want to be readmitted to it. I have lost my curiosity about the future.

Let me have back my Kharkov of old. With the torn and tattered sheepskin jacket that I wore in the winter. With my white socks. With the best breakfast in the world – bread with pickled gherkins and tea with saccharine. With the slight stuffiness resulting from closing the draught shutter in the chimney so early. With our cellar that never saw the light of day. With our own Leningrad watermelons. And the smell

* An extract from the poem "Two Captains" by Gumilyov.

[70]

of manure. And the University Garden, where I caught a swallowtail butterfly with my net. Kharkov, frozen into immobility, echoing to the sound of the railway engine whistles on the day of Lenin's death. My mother. Mayakovsky appearing live on stage. The Apollo Cinema on Moskovskaya Street. The humpback bridge across the little Lopan – where I gave some thought to committing suicide. Our dining-room table laid for Easter. A modest segment of matzo, just to taste – it won't make me into a nationalist. The Prophet Elijah, the maker of thunder. To be addressed as "Comrade", a formula I first heard in that city.

The truth, as it was known to me. The faith in which I used to believe. Give them back to me.

As chance would have it, Katya became a near neighbour – the Golovanovs set up house in Ozyorny Lane. I had been using that lane for a whole year, quite unaware of the meaning it would come to have for me once Katya moved into the house on the corner.

All the nearby streets – what had hitherto been for me a nondescript Znamenskaya, deadly dull Basseinaya – all the tram routes now led to Ozyorny Lane and came to a dead halt in front of the house on the corner.

That corner house took a long time to die in my mind, and did so slowly and piecemeal. First it was the windows that withered and fell away, then it was the turn of the main door to become defunct. Only the balcony held out in the shattered crossbeams of the memory: even now it survives, despite everything, peeling with age and forever unpopulated.

I had not previously met Katya's then husband, the actor

Astakhov. Katya must have spoken to him about me, for he greeted me as if I were an old and trusted friend.

Small, perky and spherical, with two of his front teeth missing, Igor Arkadievich Astakhov bore little resemblance to an actor. He was no more readily accepted in the Golovanov house than Tyshkevich had been. Apart from anything else, Igor earned virtually no money. He seemed to have trouble getting professional employment: it was always casual work in one or other fly-by-night theatre – its impermanency appeared not to bother him. He always had various new ideas about the theatre up his sleeve, of which I could make neither head nor tail.

Astakhov was full of goodwill toward me. It was somehow as if I merited his special trust just because I loved his wife. At times I had the impression that he was deliberately seeking by this means to impose restraint on me. As the beneficiary of his trust, I felt more of a cad than ever.

When they quarrelled, I mostly took Astakhov's side. It made no sense except insofar as we were both under Katya's spell.

In my opinion she had no idea of the torture my closeness to their family inflicted on me. My jealousy prompted me to look for bad sides to Astakhov, but I found none. I sought to comfort myself in terms of the monstrosity of Katya's character, carefully picking over all her defects and muttering aloud to myself for greater effect, but the moment I set eyes on her it all dissolved into nothing.

When things became quite unbearable, I tried to disappear from the scene, but Katya would not let me. Along would come Astakhov: "Where have you been hiding?" he would ask.

"Lots of work."

"Rubbish," Astakhov laughed. "Don't be such a fool. Come and have tea. Katya's waiting for you."

"I can't. I've exercise books to correct . . ."

He would sit down next to me on the bed, not taking his coat off. His round, kindly face shone with sympathy.

"Has she done something to offend you?"

"Not a thing."

"You know me," Astakhov said, looking me in the eyes. "You can tell me."

"But there's nothing to tell. I'm just busy: I have thirty test papers to go through."

Astakhov sighed.

"I'm fed up to the teeth with both of you. There she sits, crying because you're not there. And here you sit, going on about your exercise books. The really funny thing is that for some reason I'm supposed to sort out the relations between you! . . . Get up. Let's go!"

I got up and set off. On the way, gripping my elbow, Astakhov would appeal to me: "Don't be angry with her. She thinks the world of you."

Katya was so pleased at my turning up that I almost died with pleasure. I took tea with them, and time stood still: I needed nothing else in the world other than the table at which she was now sitting. Even Astakhov's presence failed to get me down. I had learned to comfort myself with Katya's words: "When will you at last realize that you exist independently of everyone else! Isn't that enough for you?"

She used to say it so fervently, with such conviction, that I dissolved into putty and gave in. But the moment I left her, waves of jealousy assaulted me, bouncing off the walls of the houses. That same tea table at which I had been so happy the moment before, the same Astakhov at whose little jokes I had just been laughing, and Katya too, the same Katya, but another's property, were now all tearing me into small pieces. I kept circling around Ozyorny Lane, skulking in the shadows of the houses. In the whole world just those three little windows were lit up; the main door clicked open and shut on its stiff spring; people went in and out of this building not realizing just which house they were entering and leaving: the balcony, on which my torment had imprinted its invisible mark, stood there in the sky. From horizon to horizon it was the only one for the eye to fix on. First one window went dark, then the other – that much one could just bear. The third window, in the bedroom, hurled its thunderbolt of light at me and when that light went dark, I had to pick myself up dead from the ground and crawl back to my Sapyorny Alley lodgings.

Professor Golovanov was arrested in 1930. Not the slightest thought of his being in any way guilty entered the heads of those who knew him well.

It was only much later, some six to seven years later, that the relatives and friends of those arrested came to master the horrendous art of extrapolating the offence for which one's father or mother, husband or wife, brother or sister, had disappeared.

In his frantic search to find for himself some justification for what was happening, justification not so as to survive but so as to continue living: to go on working, bringing up children, drinking, sleeping, smiling, loving, looking each other in the eye – to have the possibility and right of doing so, a person became fiendishly inventive: he sought and thought to find the reasons for the arrest.

People had worked themselves up into a fanatical faith: fanaticism always comes more readily than a rational attitude toward reality. The blind devotee begins by not asking for explanations and finishes up scornful of them.

The truth of those tragic years has become obscured. The former fanatic says with pride: yes, I was wrong, but I was in company with everyone else, with the best representatives of the people. Anyone who ventures to assert that he did realize at that time the full horror of what was going on makes himself look suspicious: he, it now appears, was guilty of not being in the wrong. He cannot be trusted: he may yet again prove the odd man out. The magic spell of the invariable rightness of the majority blinds us to all else. History knows of not a few cases when the minority was in the right.

Fyodor Ivanovich's arrest in 1930 was seen by those who knew him well as a mistake that would at any moment be corrected.

Anna Gavrilovna was never far from the telephone. She was expecting it to ring at any moment and to hear her husband had been released from prison. Katya rushed out to answer the door each time there was a ring – she had the impression that her father would suddenly appear.

No special representations were launched from the house: people had not as yet learned the perfectly useless stratagem of addressing appeals to the Great Leader – they still had faith in justice. This faith later gave way to the inhuman formula: you can't make an omelette without breaking eggs. When this proved inadequate, they changed it to: the end justifies the means.

These formulae were not vouchsafed from on high or launched from public platforms: they were painfully concocted by the people in the street in order to explain the inexplicable, to retain some faith in a life lived not entirely pointlessly.

Anna Gavrilovna took along parcels but they were not accepted – Golovanov was under interrogation. His associates at the Institute did not all drop away at once. They continued visiting Anna Gavrilovna until the rumour went around that two other prominent bacteriologists, in Kiev and in Moscow, had been arrested. According to the rumour, a group incrimination was being prepared.

The family's truest friend turned out to be someone who had not been welcome: he had paid occasional visits to them at Easter and Christmas.

Anna Gavrilovna disliked Volkov, the anatomical pathologist, for his boorishness, his alcoholic tendencies and his slovenliness. It was well known that at his lectures Professor Volkov, not always sober, would ask the girl students dubious questions on those parts of the human organism about which they were apt to be prudish. It was also well known that Volkov had drinking sessions with the watchman in the Anatomy Department.

Volkov had buried his own wife some ten years earlier. She had died of typhus and since then he had lived on his own, a gloomy, unkempt figure. His corduroy breeches were badly frayed, the heels of his shoes were always fixed on askew and there were stains on the lapels of his jacket. He would drop food from his mouth at mealtimes. In his flat two old, neglected cats survived from his wife's time. He bore traces of their fur all over him.

Volkov was not a mad eccentric. He merely lived by a different set of rules from the rest of mankind. From his long-standing involvement in the dissection theatre with dead bodies came his contempt for human vanity. Those in charge at the Institute were wary of him – his disrespect was always liable to erupt, without the least warning.

On one occasion the new, unforewarned Deputy Director summoned Volkov to see him and, among other things, politely requested Volkov to pay attention to his outward appearance.

"I'll bear it in mind." Volkov nodded his shaggy head. He gave the rubicund, prematurely corpulent, would-be-youthful-looking Deputy Director a careful look and said: "My outward appearance . . . Your autopsy would, in fact, be more repulsive than mine: a lot of fat, one would get quite mucky in it . . ."

Volkov was quite embarrassed when he came to see Anna Gavrilovna, as if he were to blame for what had happened. He uttered no words of condolence, stayed for a very short while, coughing silently. From time to time he let drop something quite inappropriate.

"Yesterday there was a nightingale singing on Krestovsky Island. It would be interesting to see how its throat is formed."

At first Anna Gavrilovna reacted coolly to his regular visits, but then grew used to them and started to worry if two days went by without him appearing.

"I must consult Anton Ignatevich," she would say, as if she had spent her whole life turning to him for advice.

Beside herself with grief, she did nothing but rush around the flat rummaging in cupboards, drawers and trunks for old photographs of Fyodor Ivanovich, for letters of his, books written by him, tributes and telegrams of congratulation sent him from all over the world on his sixtieth birthday. She laid all these trophies out in front of her in a special version of patience to which she alone had the clue, waiting for some important figure to arrive, take it all in, and then in a fury give immediate instructions for her husband to be released.

But the important figure failed to turn up, the numbers of friends now grown timid became ever greater, and there was only Volkov to whom she could endlessly lay out on display her husband's difficult and useful life.

"That's him at the time of the plague. That's during the cholera epidemic. Here he is in his Cambridge gown."

Snivelling and coughing, Volkov would look through the photos. Sometimes he would mumble: "Scoundrels."

"But why? What for?" Anna Gavrilovna would ask. "Dear Anton, I really don't understand a thing. Perhaps we need to make an approach, to say something to someone . . ."

"Mama, stop it!" Katya broke in on her. "Father is not guilty of anything. A mistake has occurred and it will be put right. You'll see, we'll be getting an official apology."

"May I get myself a vodka?" Volkov suddenly asked. He rose, went into the lobby, took a chemist's ampoule of surgical spirit out of his greatcoat pocket, looked into the kitchen, emptied the ampoule into a teacup and topped it up with one-third tap water. He was very much at home in this distraught household. Tossing back the contents, Volkov noisily sniffed at a crust of bread and munched it down.

The cupful of vodka had absolutely no effect on him.

On leaving the Golovanovs', Anton beckoned Katya to him

on the staircase: "I won't tell your mother, but I'm obliged to tell you. I urged those scoundrels at the Institute that we send in a protest. They wouldn't do it. I now refuse to shake hands with them when I meet them . . ." He brushed the tobacco ash off his greatcoat collar. "Your father has fallen ill in prison. He has uraemia. From the hunger strike he staged."

"How do you know?" asked Katya.

"Dzhanelidze told me. He performed an operation on Fyodor Ivanovich this morning. It was unsuccessful."

The next morning the interrogator telephoned Anna Gavrilovna and announced that her husband was in the surgical clinic of the Army Medical Academy: if she wished, she might visit him.

Katya went along with her mother.

Golovanov lay in a separate ward. He was unconscious. His white face above his white beard rested on a white pillow. Anna Gavrilovna failed to grasp that he could not hear her.

"Mama, you must realize . . ." Katya tried to restrain her. She stood at the foot of her father's bed so that when he came to the first thing to meet his eyes should be his daughter, not the wall.

"Leave me alone." Anna Gavrilovna waved her away. "He understands everything perfectly. Just imagine, Fedya, who we have chummed up with? With Volkov! I thought he was such a boor, but he turns out to be such a gentleman. Everyone, absolutely everyone sends greetings . . ."

In came Professor Dzhanelidze, lifted Golovanov's shrunken hand, bent over him, raised one eyelid and said to Anna Gavrilovna before even straightening up: "Your husband has died."

Golovanov's funeral was unexpectedly well attended. His death had evidently snapped the manacles of fear. His former Academy associates, doctors from all over the city who had learned their medicine from Fyodor Ivanovich's books, students – all were there. There was a doubly painful side to the funeral: the dead man was an unreleased prisoner.

When the coffin with the body inside was lifted from the bier and they were getting ready to carry it to the grave dug in the earth now rock-hard with frost, Volkov went up to the head of the Bacteriology Department, elbowed him away from the coffin and said quietly and distinctly: "Golovanov will forgive me. Get the hell out of here. Or I'll smash your skull in."

A week after the funeral I moved into Ozyorny Lane: Anna Gavrilovna had requested me to do so; she was afraid the authorities would requisition the extra living space.

I found life with the Golovanovs painful. The tragedy that brought us together had ended by taking on an everyday shape and I was inside it but not part of it.

Anna Gavrilovna's grief became the staunch cause to which she devoted her entire existence: she lived for the memory of Fyodor Ivanovich and to cultivate it by grafting onto it more and more new detail. The grief was not assumed, but strictly singled out for itself those who were parties to it and useful to it. The cause needed them as a fire needs fuel. Anything that bore no relation to her loss smacked to Anna Gavrilovna of injury and indecorum.

The regime of widow's mourning became so despotic that even Katya rebelled. She was sick at heart for her father but wanted to resume living, without marking time on the very spot at which he had perished.

Astakhov and I felt ourselves at fault in this house. He had a role – he was entitled to love Katya openly and this caused Anna Gavrilovna the minimum offence. As for me, my constant presence protected her from the unwanted intervention of the housing manager, but at the same time I served Anna Gavrilovna as a reminder of the fearful straits to which her life had been reduced.

I had the endurance and strength to put up with that – I was sorry for Anna Gavrilovna: what got me down was my no-rights situation vis-à-vis Katya.

Before my eyes, every day and every minute, Astakhov did with Katya what she and I should have been doing together. He was robbing me, stealing my last penny from me.

We spent the evenings together. I had my place at their table. Everywhere in the house I had something: my own towel in the bathroom; my own overcoat on the pegs in the lobby; my own slippers under my bed. And none of it belonged to me. The only thing that was really mine was my incessant pain.

Lying awake at night in bed, I would listen to an alien silence. I could hear Astakhov's snoring through the wall – he dared snore, lying beside Katya. There was nothing he wouldn't dare, lying at her side. When his snores suddenly petered out, life inside me came to a halt. I would bury my head in the pillow and, bruised by the silence, start to recite algebraic formulae to myself. My perfervid imagination would persist in propelling me back to the surface despite the pillows, despite the perfect logic of my solutions.

In the morning we breakfasted together.

Katya would ask: "Who are you speaking to at night?"

"To no one."

"Don't make it up, Mr Teacher." Astakhov winked·at her. "Yesterday we heard you going on about something or other."

"But that was in his sleep," said Katya. "What were you dreaming of?"

"Probably my next lesson."

"Your voice sounded strange," said Katya. "I wanted to tap on the wall but Igor wouldn't let me."

"Just his voice," said Astakhov. "Why are you so concerned about him?"

I could not carry on living that way. I arrived at school for my lesson exhausted by insomnia. It was here in class, among my pupils, that I came to my senses. The realization of my being needed put me back on my feet. This aspect of work as a teacher came to my rescue more than once. The class, the desks, the pupils' faces turned in my direction, the finite limitation of those forty-five minutes, the involuntary feeling of self-respect at the immediate prospect of having to undertake an important feat – it all took me by the scruff of the neck and gave me a proper shaking. I got on with the lesson.

Behind me, shoulder to shoulder, stood a line of decent, long-revered educationalists: Shaposhnikov, Valtsev, Kiselyov and Rybkin. Judged against the exactitude of the truths they sought to impart, my torment was a relative matter. I was put in my place by Shaposhnikov and Valtsev, Kiselyov and Rybkin. In essence, I was still a semi-educated upstart – the achievement of the authors of the textbooks inspired infinite respect in me.

[82]

The rudimentary mathematics I then knew continues even now to arouse my admiration. Worlds come and go, entire nations go wild, historical eras betray themselves, but parallel lines continue to meet only in infinity.

Please, fly to the moon, synthesize the albumen, but do leave my parallel lines alone. For an old, tired man must have one truth to which he can cling.

And so I found myself in the Urals in the city of Sverdlovsk – in 1931 it still remembered its old name, Ekaterinburg.

It all happened in a rush.

On the announcements board in the corridor of my Timiryazev School someone had pinned up a notice announcing that the regional committee of the teachers' union was recruiting volunteers for work in educational establishments in the Urals.

I really didn't mind where I went or whom I taught. I just had to disappear. I did not then appreciate that there is no such option, for, wherever you disappear to, life's impedimenta will slowly but surely catch up with you.

This time I knew that Katya would shed no tears over my departure. She had other things on her mind. Impending exams, frequent rows with her mother, Astakhov's inability to settle down to work – all these things preoccupied her.

On learning that I had put my name down to go, she said: "Well, maybe you're right."

The bitterness welled up in me. I replied: "Let's leave the details till you write."

"Heavens, what a nasty piece of work you are! Why are you so bitter about it?"

"Pay no attention. Pure nerves. Resulting from prolonged

abstention. I'll get over it in Sverdlovsk – I'll see to that."

"You won't dare," said Katya.

"I shall. Now I know how it's done. I've learned a lot, lying on my side of your wall."

"I hate you," Katya said.

"It's of no great consequence," I replied.

The train left at six in the evening. In the early morning, while the house was still asleep, I endeavoured to pack.

A large wicker basket lay astride two chairs. My things were strewn all around, on the floor, on the bed and on the window ledges. I tried cramming them in one by one as they came to hand, but when the basket was full to the brim, half my stuff still remained littered around the room. I felt desperate to drop it all and leave, bearing just what I stood up in. This flat had got the better of me.

"Chevalier de Grieux," I said to myself, "you silly little shit."

The basket refused to shut. I sat on its creaking lid and with difficulty fastened the catches.

The Sverdlovsk Educational Authority assigned me to the Ural-Siberian Communist University. I acquired the title of Assistant Teacher in the Faculty of Mathematics. My lessons were henceforward called lectures.

These authoritative terms – university, faculty, lecture – appealed to my burgeoning vanity: it seems that I was for the first time taking myself seriously as a professional.

A sense of pedagogical exhilaration overcame me. This feeling was induced by the fact that in my Communist University I could deploy the entire sum of my knowledge, omitting nothing. All the scraps of information I had picked up in the course of my life could be fed into my work as if into a bottomless pit. There was only a modest hoard of them and, after giving my lectures, I used to return to my rooms in the University hostel drained and exhausted.

The level of knowledge among the Communist University students was so low that even my rudimentary self-education appeared to them to be the snowy summits of an unscalable mountain range. Officials from local Party committees, from rural and factory Party cells, chairmen of village soviets and district executive committees, all getting on in years, sat before me in the former mansion of the millionaire Demidov and strove not to miss a single word of the fearfully meagre stock of learning which I lavishly doled out to them.

The boyhood years of my "mature students" had been spent in the countryside and the villages. They had learned to read and write from the village priest, in their local church school, and in the three-year urban colleges. It was out of the question to bridge the yawning gap between their experience of life and their educational backwardness. The Communist University sought to span this gulf with flimsy pontoons hastily assembled from whatever material was available. By careful equilibration, one could just walk across them.

It was easier for me than for the other instructors. I did not have to squat down to be on a level with my students: I drew myself up to my full height. Their pious attitude toward mathematics did not seem to me naïve. The successful division of decimal fractions reduced them to a state of ecstasy which I shared. To me it was a miracle that I was able to teach them anything.

The method I used to put this over was one invented by

me, completely on my own. My students did not comprehend abstract notions. And I wanted at all costs to be understood. Demonstrating an inhuman ingenuity, I attempted to find a practical daily equivalent for each mathematical concept.

"And where do you apply it in practice, in daily life?" my students kept asking.

The question did not offend me. At that time I considered it quite natural. It seemed to me axiomatic that even political events could be visualized as an aspect of mathematics. I devised exercises on industrial, defence and agricultural themes. I had exercises on "wrecking", on "Party deviations".

I was convinced that mathematics was a class science. Such a standpoint was much in demand, and I genuinely shared and propagated it. My students' eyes lit up with unholy zeal when I told them how there was a kulak brand of mathematics and another for the factory workers in alliance with the poorest peasants.

I dug out from Engels' *Anti-Dühring* and *Dialectics of Nature* three or four examples handy for substantiating my approach. Friedrich himself was an unwitting accomplice.

Looking back to that period, I would like to be able to record with particular care my general attitude at the time. However, it is difficult for me now to overlook the fact that the tendency to become blinded by belief was already taking root in people's minds. The trouble, as I see it, is that belief directed like the beam of headlights at the road ahead of you lights up only an infinitesimal portion of the journey you have to undertake, while if directed straight into your eyes it will blind you. Headlights of that period hit you right between the eyes, head on.

[86]

That at least was the case with me. The peak period of my fallibility was 1930. That is not to say I subsequently had no trouble in distinguishing what was good from what was base. It was simply that I began to allow myself the privilege of making my own mistakes. Which meant, incidentally, that my awakening was all the more painful.

Our University hostel site was under construction some five miles from Sverdlovsk.

There, amid the bare fields of the virgin steppe, enormous, cumbersome accommodation blocks were being thrown up in a hurry. There were no intervening streets, and the whole lot looked like a vast gypsy encampment made out of bricks assembled under the open sky. The six-storey "tents" were like a multicoloured patchwork quilt: the base was red brick, above that was whatever came to hand – grey or white or yellow stone.

There was an absence of door and window catches or handles, and frames were jammed fast with four-inch nails, the doors hung crookedly on lengths of leather and did not reach the floor: the floor planking, from newly felled pine, creaked as it dried out and ended up jutting proudly. The untamed Ural winds howled in under the window ledges and brought the plasterwork crumbling down onto the floor. The wind foraged along the long, semi-dark corridor – the only source of light for which was two small windows set into the woodwork.

The students started the process of settling into the half-finished housing blocks of the University "campus" amid the dust, the racket, the chaos of construction. Meanwhile

[87]

the upper storeys were being superimposed over their heads, the floor under their feet was having the planking added to it, and the rusty water in the pipes rose only as far as the third floor. Monumental cast-iron troughs ran the full length of the narrow washrooms with handbasins equipped with drain plugs above them. The smell of ammonia was strong enough to bring tears to your eyes and make you choke.

I was happy. I had been given a room on the fifth floor of one of the University blocks. My window, which extended the full length of the wall, was divided by small panes and had a view of Lake Shartash in the distance. The mist from the lake seeped through all the cracks and settled overnight on my standard-issue flannel blanket.

I was happy. I had things to do to occupy my mind. I had people around me who needed me. And in response I loved them.

In my picture of the world of that time they were people who had mastered something of which I had only a hazy notion. Their dedication, determination and intelligence seemed to me of statesmanlike proportions. I saw in them ascetics who were sacrificing their wellbeing for the sake of the good of the people.

Soaked to the skin by the fierce Ural downpours, half buried in the snow, up to their ankles in mud and to their knees in the snowdrifts, or with the acrid dust from the steppes whipping at their faces, they faced a walk of up to five kilometres from our block to the campus proper on National Revenge Square. They came back to their hostel accommodation in the growing dark. The miserly allowance they received barely sufficed, on a minimal hand-to-mouth basis, to keep them from starving. There was nothing to buy in the city shops. An entire wall of tins rose vertically behind the backs of assistants, whom abandon had rendered quite eccentric. There were pyramids of the same tins in the windows. They were labelled: DISPLAY ONLY.

The newspapers proclaimed that soya and margarine were healthier than meat or butter. Neither soya nor margarine was on sale. Scientists demonstrated from experimenting on rats that a generous intake of food was harmful: where food was concerned, abstinence was proper. That year Sverdlovsk ate "properly".

It never occurred to any of us in the University hostel that things could be any different. We spooned our thin cabbage soup into our mouths in the students' canteen, drank our mugs of hot, murky, w/s (without sugar) tea and, head in the clouds, inhaled the rarefied air of the future.

I do not recall ever having such a sense of my own rightness as I did then. The immediate utility of my teaching work doubled my zeal. Our students started from zero, so their level of knowledge registered an immediate, plainly observable improvement.

It was much later that one general aspect of their intellectual progress became clear to me. When people in their thirties and forties manage to learn what they should by rights have learned as children and what children learn as a matter of course, in their stride, without expending any vast mental effort on doing so, those no longer young, burdened down by their experience of life, find it a dramatic experience: the last-minute acquisition of elementary knowledge burrows deep into their skull, making them dogmatic and resistant to the subsequent absorption of knowledge on a more advanced plane. They find it difficult to renounce what they so laboriously acquired. And they treat with much too much respect those simplistic, banal ideas which they mastered at an uncomfortably advanced age.

Even many years later, even today, I am occasionally able to identify former Communist University students of mine among people with whom I happen to fall into conversation. I recognize them precisely because of their way of thinking. The most capable and influential of our students sometimes found jobs with the Institute of Red Professors or the Industrial Academy, achieved influential posts or, from time to time, became good servants of the state, but many of them bore the same general stamp. They tended to see the world in terms of black and white. Its wide variety of colour found no place in their perception. Their approach to the complex problems of science and art, and life too, for that matter, was oversimplified, sometimes crassly so.

For a long time I too could distinguish only two colours – black and white.

There were two of us assigned to my room in the University hostel: I and a mathematics teacher named Arseny Georgievich Posmysh.

Posmysh was stupid. He had an appalling habit of gesticulating in the air with his finger as if writing on a blackboard. When talking to you, he would describe circles around your face with the middle finger of his right hand. Posmysh used the tactic to impart his lacklustre thoughts in both verbal and written communication. The mere sight of his fingertip in motion was enough to send me to sleep.

Yet for all that, his handsome, distinguished, impressive face was set off by a pair of ironic lips. It was a mystery how, from what unfair combination of genes, Posmysh had become the possessor of the fine, sardonic traits of a sceptic. Perhaps in randomly acquiring them he had disinherited some polymath condemned to go around with the alien (to him), triumphantly stupid face of Posmysh.

I know that I was unjust to him. It now worries me that I found him so irritating then. Posmysh taught mathematics better than I. He loved his subject and had an excellent knowledge of it. But I found sharing with him, and his acute need of company, extremely painful.

He kept a diary in a thick, linen-covered notebook. He never lowered himself to recording the petty events of everyday life in his diary. The diary was for thoughts. Excerpts from the books of great thinkers had the effect on Posmysh of high-tension wires: they brought about a series of short circuits in his mind and burned out before reaching his conscious awareness. Their current passed through him and away into the earth.

The broad margins of the diary were generously annotated in Posmysh's hand:

Nota bene.
Quite right.
Dubious.
Remember to use in practice.
Think about at leisure.

I lived for three months in the same room with him. His good sense, his pedantry, and even his benevolence irritated me.

In the morning he would ask me: "I hope your night's sleep has made a fresh man of you?"

And before going to bed he would write in the air with his middle finger: "Permit me to wish you pleasant dreams."

He was, to me, an offensively sound sleeper, and when he woke up, he smiled.

In all probability I must have envied him his stability of temperament. Sometimes I found myself wanting to make him lose his temper, but I never succeeded in doing so. His response to my rudeness was to say: "You are angry, Jupiter, so you must be in the wrong."

I think he was probably sorry for me. I think he was genuinely sorry for anyone who did not resemble him. It was sympathy welling out of incomprehension.

He liked to say to me: "In your place, I would . . ."

"You won't be in my place!" I retorted.

Posmysh was ten years older than I. So I knew for a fact that he couldn't be in my place. And it was not so enviable a place at that.

When Valya Snegiryova came to join me from Kharkov, Arseny Georgievich put on his best suit. He was more excited than I was. I had announced to him a month before Valya's arrival that I was getting married.

"I congratulate you with my whole heart," said Posmysh. "I hope Hymen's bonds will not impede our staunch friendship." Without any prompting on my part, he went straight off to the hospital administrator and asked to be assigned lodgings in someone else's room.

[92]

"If you need money to get settled in," Posmysh offered, "my purse is at your disposal."

The very first evening he called in to see us, highly excited: without crossing the threshold, he handed Valya a bouquet of flowers.

"I wish you and your husband," said Posmysh, "every happiness in your personal life and creative success in your work."

This super-pompous formula had then not yet been officially launched. But Posmysh had an astounding ability to anticipate banalities, even those still to be given currency.

He was good to me. And especially to Valya. He failed to notice that Valya's eyes were red with crying, but expressed admiration for everything she did; for her strong tea, the curtains at the windows, and the cupboard she bought for our room. He would take Valya to the cinema and, on bringing her home, would say to me: "I hope you're not jealous?"

He read out to her extracts from his beloved diary.

In his continuing enthusiasm for our domestic bliss, he did not notice my or Valya's growing sense of isolation.

Sasha Belyavsky told you the truth, Zinaida Borisovna; I treated Valya badly.

That is how I see it now: not how I saw it then.

In those days I considered that marriages were made not in heaven but in bed. Nowadays I, doubtless as you do, tell young people that one's initial passion gives way to something deeper – to friendship, community of souls, shared responsibility. But if only the Lord would allow one to re-experience just once that total careless rapture which kindles young love

[93]

into a red-hot glow. May I, dear Lord, flutter in that flame just one more time.

Valya had just completed her course of study at the local musical training college in Sverdlovsk, having come here from Kharkov to do her final year. On graduating she had been assigned to a teaching job in an orphans' school. The work of a music teacher did not appeal to her. Given the relationship between us, it was doubtful whether work of any sort would have distracted her.

We didn't quarrel. I was, it seemed to me, considerate with her. A few days before her arrival I had with some difficulty found a lady who undertook to bring us milk three times a week. At that time it cost an enormous amount of money. The milk was delivered punctually. Choking back her tears, Valya drank the damned stuff. The more I felt at fault before Valya, the more effort I put into taking care of her. That too is a form of caddishness.

At night when we went to bed, Valya always had cold legs. On light summer nights I would see her sleeping with her mouth open. Had I loved her, I would have found this touching. What shameful minutiae go to make up the sense of estrangement you come to feel toward the person with whom you are sleeping.

We did not quarrel. Quarrels are only conceivable when you can put a name to the cause. We had no possibility of doing so.

After ten to twelve hours a day lecturing, I was dead on my feet: my daily life was a constant sleepwalk. Teaching parallel classes reduced me to a state of idiocy: I had to parrot the same thing four times a day. By the evening, from sheer fatigue the faces of my students had all merged into one impersonal blur and I had the impression of having given one and the same explanation to one and the same person ever since morning. On my way home to my hostel quarters I would mechanically continue the same processes in my mind, totting up the numbers of the houses and the trams. I was happy when they came out to a round figure.

When autumn came the University lecture theatres suddenly emptied: the students were all spirited away, as if in response to an invisible alarm system, to work in the fields. On returning, it took them some time to recover themselves: their tired eyes continued to show traces of the frenzy built up by their stint of sheer hard physical labour.

In my free time, when I was not lecturing, I worked at putting together a Problem-and-Answer Reader for the University. The job had been assigned to me by the Scientific Workers section of our University. I was proud of the assignment. I was convinced it would be a success and was impatient for an ovation from my faculty. I ventured so far out to sea on the stormy swell of my vanity that I was already visualizing the award of a postgraduate degree.

It so happened that the Rector was present at our faculty meeting which was due to sanction my Reader project. I had not met him before. From University rumour, I knew that the Rector was an Old Bolshevik who had been disciplined for some sort of deviation and, in disgrace, had been seconded from Moscow to us in Sverdlovsk.

The lecturers sat around a long table. The Rector's frail figure, seated obliquely from me, was lost from sight among them. I remember being struck by his large shaggy head. He sat with it inclined toward the table.

I gave the faculty a glib account of the principle behind the composition of my Reader. The entire book would be based on present-day material. The growth of the students' political awareness would acquire a solid mathematical backing. I quoted, by way of illustration, one or two bang up-to-date examples. One of them was the Syrtsov-Lominadze Opposition.

The Rector chimed in quietly: "That's all so incredibly vulgar and simplistic."

In the suddenly ensuing silence I asked provocatively: "In other words, you consider that mathematics needs to be isolated from reality?"

"That's an idiotic question," said the Rector.

Something snapped inside me. I felt outrage and injury. I dropped back into my chair, scanning the faces of my comrades with perplexed eyes. They were silent, and avoided my gaze. Only Posmysh passed me a hasty note across the table: "I'm morally on your side."

That same evening I submitted notice of my resignation to the Head of the faculty. On reading it, she sighed: "The Rector displayed a lack of tact."

"Offensiveness," I said. "Insolence."

"You shouldn't react so intemperately," said the faculty Head. "The Rector has big problems; he's on edge . . . I shall keep your application by me. Do give it further thought."

Years went by in which I failed to manage to give the matter further thought. For a long time I nursed in my heart the injury inflicted on me by the Rector. Compassion for the old man and piercing shame at myself only came to me much, much later.

In 1965 I happened to find myself staying in the same rest house as Lominadze's widow. On being introduced to this now elderly lady who had difficulty in turning her head as a result of the interrogations she had endured, I recalled the little test problem I had devised thirty-five years earlier. With the aid of a few figures, I had sought to demonstrate that Lominadze was an enemy of the people.

I had demonstrated it. They had had him shot.

* * *

The thirst for absolution is unquenchable. Plagued by it, we inflict on each other shameless details from our sordid lives. Now contrite, as if confronting death, we carry on living, casting glances of amazement back at the maimed stump of our past.

I know I am being unjust to it. There is something wrong with my memory's focus: it registers a distorted picture of the past.

I stroll backward, placing my feet in my own tracks, heelprint to heelprint. And at the halfway mark I bump into myself striding forward.

Nowadays we recognize each other at once.

I take a step to one side, silently making way for him.

"The last time," he says, "there was something you wanted to warn me about."

"It's pointless. There's nothing you can change."

"Even if I know it beforehand?"

"Even so."

"Rubbish," he says. "Armed with a precise knowledge of the future, I would know how to act."

"And with that knowledge you would act in precisely the same way as those without it. Only, things would become much more difficult for you."

"But that contradicts science." He starts getting annoyed.

"Maybe."

He sweeps past me. I feel sorry for him and shout after him: "You'll survive!"

Katya's letters reached me at my home address in Sverdlovsk. They were few and far between. I wrote to her that I had married, but Katya notified me, en passant, that she considered my marriage invalid.

She never once wrote to me in a tranquil frame of mind. The palpitation in her letters conveyed itself to me too as soon as I handled the envelope. I did not have the patience to open it neatly. I was never able to take in the contents of a letter from her on first perusal. Choking on her words, like a starving man on bread, I would force them down in enormous chunks, at first taking in no more than their overall sound. The sound they made inside me was that of Katya's voice.

. . . In the 1942 winter blockade of Leningrad letters from her reached me from Tashkent. They were a long time in arriving – months, in fact. The lorries transporting them had become half sunk in the ice of frozen Lake Ladoga. The ink had run from contact with the water. Individual words impacted on me like a cry for help. Some of the envelopes had written on their reverse: "Comrades Postmen! Comrades

Military Censors! Please ensure that this letter reaches my husband – I cannot live without him."

I was to blame.

I had caused her to leave Leningrad on the first evening of the war.

My hurt at her agreeing to leave and her hurt at my not leaving with her clashed together that evening at the railway station. We still had no idea of the dimensions of the calamity that was about to overtake us. No one yet had. Each individual pain was like a narcosis preventing one from sensing its universality, its wholeness.

The crowded station was silent as if for a funeral. The last Red Arrow was departing. On that first day of war, suddenly everything became the last of its kind.

The last Katya stood on the steps of the coach.

How very many years have had to go by before I got my love for her completely out of my system.

There will never be a second Batiliman.

I told the sanatorium director that we were husband and wife and that we needed a room to ourselves.

"That's a rotten thing to do," Katya said angrily. "I'll go and see him this very moment and tell him you made it all up."

The director had gone off somewhere and there was no sign of him before evening came and then it grew dark, and the small house in which we had been allotted a room to ourselves disappeared from sight in the cloud that had swept down from the mountain.

I stayed up all night, fully dressed, in a wicker chair, with my suitcase standing unpacked in the corner. There were two bunks in the room. Katya slept in one of them. From time to time she woke up and would mutter: "Serves you right . . . You shouldn't have fibbed."

And so it went on for seven days and seven nights.

In the mornings we made our way to the sea, down to a deserted bay. It had all somehow happened before. There I was, scrambling down the rock crevices, grabbing at the arid bushes for a handhold. There was nothing in the wide world to concern me – the sea and the cliffs were too immortal and too boundless for me to be able to appreciate trifles a mere thousand years old.

Grilled by the sun, we lay on the hot flat rocks with the sea salt settling on our skin in a white spray. We had created this earth and had not yet contrived to populate it.

On the eighth night Katya called me over to her. Time fragmented and ceased to exist. Space became non-existent except for that part of it under my hand. The whole sense and purpose of my life fitted into that narrow sanatorium bunk. Before it was nothing, and after it would be nothing. There was only this. My senses saturated to the point of suffocation, I died and was reborn. I died again and was reborn again.

When we went into the room, it was knee-deep in a warm haze redolent with the scent of wormwood which had been strewn over the floor as a protection against bugs. We trampled across it in our bare feet, and drank water straight out of the jug, letting it stream over our bodies. The water jug stood on the windowsill and when we went to it the sleep-weary voices of the cicadas called out in our direction. Then the dawn made

[100]

its diffident entry through the wide-open window, escorted inside our room by a gentle early-morning breeze. The haze, like a foggy mist, rose to the ceiling, swirled around the corners of the room, and suddenly vanished. That part of the twenty-four-hour day, which had up till then passed me by, had an aroma and a colour unknown to me: it seemed that it even had its own sound register, a delicate, barely detectable one. "Now I'm done for," said Katya.

"That would be nice," I said. "Done for good, I hope."

"I always knew it would end this way. And you?"

"I didn't know a damned thing. And would I have dared know? If I had really known, would I have stuck it all those years?"

"Listen to you, three years," said Katya. "If someone really loves, he will wait his whole life long."

"And after that?" I asked.

It grew completely light in the room. We were feeling astonishingly relaxed after our sleepless night. A large mosquito with long, bare legs, looking like a ballerina, settled on Katya's hand.

"Don't kill him," Katya begged. "You know what's so strange? Everything that used to seem important now seems meaningless. But the trivial things to which I used to pay no attention have suddenly become overwhelming. Do you feel the same?"

"Of course," I said. "I've developed a second sight and a second hearing."

"It's funny that you once taught me physics. I still remember Gay-Lussac's law."

"He was a good lad, was Gay-Lussac," I said.

"But wasn't it two lads?" Katya asked. "I thought there was Gay and there was Lussac."

"You've mixed it up with Boyle and Mariotte."

"Were they married?" asked Katya.

"Boyle was in love with Mariotte's wife. He was mad about her. In essence, it was Mariotte who devised his famous law. And he tacked Boyle's name on out of pure fellow feeling."

"You've only just made that up," said Katya. "Make something else up and I'll lie down with my eyes closed."

She closed her eyes and I improvised: "Let's stay here for ever."

"In Batiliman?" Katya asked in a sleepy voice.

"I'll get myself a job as court jester. And in the winter, when they're all gone, they'll re-employ me as a stoker."

"There are no furnaces here," Katya said.

"I'll build Dutch ovens. You can't imagine what I'm capable of."

"How about the wood?"

"I'll plant a wood."

"A pine wood?"

"Whatever kind you want."

After three weeks, when our holiday passes had run out, she left for Kiev to rejoin her husband: Astakhov was having a poor time of it there with some touring company.

I accompanied her as far as Kharkov. I needed to go further, to Sverdlovsk, but I had no money left for the ticket. I didn't want to ask Father for it. I was told in the Blood Transfusion Institute that they paid donors three hundred roubles for five hundred grams of blood. At that time they were bad at storing blood properly and resorted to direct transfusion from donor to recipient.

Fortunately for me some nutcase at the local psychiatric hospital had chosen that day to smash in the window with his fist and had severed a vein. We were put on adjacent tables in the operating theatre. My half litre of blood, full of my Batiliman frenzy, was pumped into the nutcase. I was paid three hundred roubles and given a blood donor's ration: half a kilo of granulated sugar and a kilogram of oatmeal. Are you still alive, my beloved loony? You really did help me out. Please forgive me, by the way, for the muck they pumped into your vein from mine.

I bought a ticket to Sverdlovsk, but on the way there, in Moscow, I got out of the train, made my way to Sukharevka, opened my suitcase and stood in line with the stall-holders at the market. After flogging off the contents of my suitcase, I bought a ticket to Kiev.

"Why have you come?" Katya asked me. "Igor knows everything and has forgiven me."

We were standing on Vladimir Hill, on the narrow bridge above the valley. Far below, down by the Dnieper, Astakhov was strolling along with his back to us. I recognized his short, hateful figure.

"I can just see you," I said, "cringing at his feet, imploring forgiveness."

"But I love him," said Katya.

"What in the hell induced you to sleep with me in Batiliman?"

"Don't torture me," Katya implored. "People have the misfortune of loving two different persons."

"They do," I roared. "With whores, damn you, anything can happen!"

When I ran down the hill from the bridge, she did not come after me, did not call me back, did not weep out loud.

I looked back to see her slowly making her way down to the river. Astakhov was walking toward her, his face transfigured by a look of pathetic happiness.

Sofia Lvovna, the Russian-language teacher at the school where I was studying, asked my mother to come and see her.

"Tell me, please," Sofia Lvovna asked, "does your boy live at home in normal conditions."

"In what I consider normal ones," my mother replied.

"Have you by chance noticed any strange behaviour on his part?"

"Nothing in particular," said Mother. "He's not very good at washing his feet before he goes to bed, but I make him do so."

"Do you beat him?"

"Not in the literal sense. Of course, sometimes he needs to be given the odd pinch. Has he done something at school?"

"You see," said Sofia Lvovna, "your son writes very sad compositions. On the last occasion the class was asked to write an essay on 'how I spent the summer'."

"We spent the summer in Pokatilovka," my mother said. "They were pretty short of foodstuffs there."

"It's not the food he complains of," said Sofia Lvovna. "In fact, he complains of nothing. He's a happy child. But his compositions are all rather gloomy in a way unusual for his age."

Mama wanted to protect me. She said: "Maybe he has tapeworms. I'll try and keep an eye on him."

*

I did not have worms. Why I filled my exercise books with mournful stories, I don't know. For that matter, it was much later I noticed that in Russia only gloomy men write humorous stories.

I always had the impression that there was something due to happen later, or about to happen. I never thought that whatever was my current way of life would last very long. Even now, at the age of sixty, I don't have the feeling of permanency in this world of ours.

Maybe things will yet turn out differently from the way they have turned out so far. I do not know whether many people have the idea that their life is a matter of pure chance. Maybe it is something typical of the time we live in? Maybe, however weird the form a man's fate assumes, there is a common trait in the way he seeks to rediscover his past?

In trying to assess how I related to my surroundings, I come up with very meagre findings. Or, rather, I do not know what scale of measurement to apply, where my starting point should be. I am unable to measure the modalities: it might have happened this way, it might have happened that way.

As with everyone else, there were quite a number of occasions on which I might have died – but I didn't. That was not my fault, nor was it to my credit. So the main conclusion I deduce is that nothing ever depended on me.

Who are we? – my generation, that is.

At crisis points in our epoch, this notion of a generation becomes foreshortened. The relief contingent, as in battle, is required to appear on the scene at ever shorter intervals. The untested raw recruits give the veterans an ironic look. But it's not like that at the front.

[105]

A generation, tortured by insomnia.

We performed our greatest feats in the early morning, lying in bed with our eyes open. Fearless and chivalrous, we rushed headlong into battle in the name of justice. The unfurled banners of our conscience streamed out proudly in the wind of truth. Wriggling inside our sweaty sheets in the profound dark of night, we delivered accusatory speeches. How many such speeches for the prosecution, these night-time orations, did I pronounce to the loud pitter-patter of my heartbeat? The outer doors of the highest offices in the land swung wide open at my behest. The public platforms at once emptied themselves of orators so as to make way for me. I never had to ask. The simplicity of my night-time logic rested on the premise that decent people should have things made easy for them and bad people should have a hard time of it. I released people from prison, brought slanderers to justice, stripped hidebound hypocrites and cynics of their ration entitlements. The pure truth, acting like surgical spirits, kept me at night in a state of permanent intoxication. I kept tossing it back inside me till I became totally befuddled.

Who are we? – my generation, that is.

Dreamers of the twenties, much thinned out in number and tortured in the thirties, reduced to a pulp in the forties, emasculated by blind faith yet not restored to strength by the prospect of a dawn, we pursue our own individual peregrination. We are not good at finding common ground. Looking at each other, as if in a mirror, we are astounded at our own disfigurement.

But we wanted it all for the best.

*

Memories are kittle cattle. For a time they lie hidden, and live inside you in haphazard clusters which all of a sudden cascade down on you in a completely random torrent bearing no relation whatsoever to what is happening to you.

A large Uzbek led the way. He walked with an easy, broad step despite my heavy baggage: he carried the soft bale containing Katya's things on his massive shaven head and switched the long, heavy suitcase from one hand to the other as he went.

The Uzbek kept looking back at me with a smile that spread right across his face. I had given him the address – 15 Engels Street – inside the railway station, and now he was confidently guiding me through the warm streets of Tashkent.

It was evening and the city was already recovering from the heat. The delicate evanescent smell of greenery coming to life came wafting in over the nauseous stench of evacuation centres, overheated railway carriages and station termini.

After paying the Uzbek off at the house, I squatted down on the porch and unwrapped the rags that enveloped my swollen feet. The rags were stuffed into capacious galoshes and pulled together with string.

The house was asleep.

Five windows were lit in its single-storey façade.

I attempted to guess which one was Katya's. Oddly enough, I experienced no sense of manic urgency. I could in fact have continued sitting on the porch, amid these strangely but pleasantly unreal surroundings. The year spent in the siege of Leningrad had put an end to all my impatience. It had driven all passion out of my body. Other than a passionate desire to survive.

[107]

Lyusya answered my knock. The fat lady is called Lyusya, Katya had written in her letter to me.

"Oh, you've come! But Katya's out at supper."

Her plump, sleepy face seemed to close up. We took my baggage into the house.

Lyusya did not put on the light in the room which we entered, but I realized from the smell that it was Katya's. Everything that took place that night only gradually filtered through to my conscience in dribs and drabs. Perhaps this was my overexhausted body deploying its defences: it allowed through only those emotions with which it could cope.

A streetlamp dimly lit the room and I looked cautiously round it. Various of Katya's things – a dress hanging on a nail, house slippers, a warm check scarf – met my eyes. But it was a no-man's-room in the sense of what we understand by no-man's-land.

Next to a tidily folded-away bed was someone's photograph standing in a frame on top of a bedside table. Fat Lyusya tried to shield it from my gaze with a hasty twitch of her large bottom.

I sat down on a narrow sofa, without taking off my overcoat.

"Perhaps you would like to have a wash after your journey; I'll pour the water for you," said Lyusya.

I took off my coat and asked for it to be put out in the yard – there might be train bugs in it.

The photograph showed the torso of a man in a clean white shirt with a tie. The cigarette in his mouth was not hand-rolled but properly, professionally made.

I did my washing over an aluminium bowl in the passage-way, while Lyusya poured water over me from a jug. She stared at the black water streaming down from my hands and my face. I really wanted to wash right down to my waist, but I knew that the lower part of my vest had stuck to the boils that had burst open on my back – warm water was needed to ease it free in those places.

But there was still no sign of Katya.

I was not worried by this – it was Lyusya who was worrying. From nervousness, the source of which I could not understand, she talked incessantly. I hardly bothered to try and make sense of what she was saying. When we returned from the passageway to the room, the photograph was no longer there; presumably, Lyusya had managed to spirit it away.

That too was a matter of indifference to me. I could not properly think anything through. Thinking things through to a conclusion can be fatal. One must not think back, or think ahead – that was what I had taught myself in besieged Leningrad.

There was still no sign of Katya. A clock struck the hour in the next room.

"Heavens," said Lyusya. "It's midnight already. I'll go and meet her."

We both set off, with me tagging behind Lyusya. It looked as if she didn't want me with her, but I was past caring.

We met Katya somewhere along the road: she was on her way home. Lyusya spotted her first. On seeing her, she ran in Katya's direction and gabbled something which I could not make out and did not even try to. I had the impression of still being in Leningrad and here was someone else walking along a street in Tashkent, a someone who was of very little concern to me. I was happy for him – the sands of time were not running out, the shells were not exploding around him, some two hours back he had scoffed a whole loaf of bread in his train compartment.

Katya paused and listened to the fat lady. And I continued walking toward them, head high, body taut.

"Hallo," I said when I got to them.

"Who are you?" Katya asked.

"You've gone mad," said the fat lady. "It's Boris!"

"I don't know who Boris is," said Katya.

We walked side by side.

That's it, then, I thought, dully. It's not so complex after all.

The enormity of what had just happened was more than I could take in. It lay there in a crumpled heap beside me. I could see that it had collapsed, but for the very reason that it had subsided so incoherently and so suddenly I felt no cosmic shock.

For all that it was a knock-out blow – I don't remember how we got back to the house. Lyusya had disappeared. Katya plugged in the electric element, lowered it into a jug of water, but when the water boiled we forgot to make ourselves tea.

I asked her: "Is he the man whose photo you had on your table?"

"Yes," Katya said.

"A long time?"

"Six months."

"Why on earth didn't you write to me?"

"I resisted doing so," said Katya. "I thought it would pass."

"You must have had it bad, not even recognizing me."

"That's not why," Katya said. "I had been smoking hashish.

He left for good a week ago. For Warsaw. He's a Pole . . .
Dear God, if only you knew how bad I feel. I'm quite unable
to cope on my own . . ."
    "Not everyone's able," I said.
    "I was entirely on my own. I was so lonely . . ."
    "And he took pity on you?"
    "He was very sorry for me."
    I asked: "How often each night was he sorry for you?"

I left Sverdlovsk abruptly. At that age I did everything suddenly. The distance between an incipient urge and action was
negligible. I was only aware then of one means of salvation
from life's aggravations – to take to one's heels. One had to
drop everything. And get the hell out of it. And then start
again. I had the idea that a new set of circumstances would
make a new man of me.
    When we are young we see ourselves as more idiosyncratic
than we are. We are incapable of appreciating our similarity
to others. We think we are far from being typecast. We play
up our individuality and our self-sufficiency. How sad it is
that with the years we lose this feeling. With the years the
yoke of conformity wrings our withers till they bleed. And the
blowflies of the daily round, the common task, hover over our
open wounds.
    Why can't you be content with what you've got? Why do
you need more than others?
    I don't need more than others.
    Now once more I find myself strolling through Leningrad.
I have no lodgings, no money, and I am twenty-five years old.
    I roam the streets, studying the notices in front of the edu-

cational establishments. The times are oddly out of joint, as yet uninfected by the poison of "vigilance". Kirov has not yet been assassinated. I am taken on straight "off the street" as a mathematics teacher in a military college.

I am allocated a room of my own in the officers' hostel. I am issued some blue material to be made up into breeches, a length of green serge for my officer's jacket, cloth for a heavy greatcoat and polished leather to be made into boots. Two pairs of white cotton drawers complete my military outfit.

I am not an officer. I am a civilian volunteer. I am called "Comrade Teacher", but I am supposed to be saluted. When I appear at the entrance to the classroom, all the cadets' boots snap together in a single thunderous clap as they rise to their feet behind their desks – the class leader delivers his report to me, holding himself rigidly at attention.

I find playing at being a soldier pleases me. My uniform collars are without badges of rank. In the army store I buy myself two bars and, after pinning one to each of the two collars of my jacket, I go to the cinema.

I was scared to go through to the auditorium but, overcoming my nerves, I managed to saunter around two or three times among the crowd. I had the impression that the casual civilian loungers were struck with admiration at the taut military officer's figure.

It was in this martial attire in the small Footlights cinema that I was confronted by the college's Chief of Staff, Divisional Commander Lvov. Brought up nose to nose with him, I took a step back and put my hand to my throat so as to hide from him the purchased bars on my collars. He glanced severely at me in my sudden state of immobility and moved on.

[112]

I do come across him nowadays, a decrepit, gaunt little old man who holds himself as straight as a rod. In the bookshops. He is holding out a book at arm's length, at a safe distance from his own prying eyes, and slowly leafing through it beside the bookshelves. I have noticed: more often than not it is a book of poetry.

He was an unsociable, acerbic person, both respected and feared in our college. I still retain my feeling of diffidence and respect for him to this day.

Comrade Chief of Staff, Divisional Commander Lvov! May I have a word with you thirty years after the events in question?

Perhaps you should not have chucked me out of the college? By the time it happened I had been working for you for three years. My relations with the cadets were good. Despite my completely unprofessional methods, I taught them certainly no worse than the other teachers. Maybe even better. The immaturity of my pedagogical know-how was offset by love. Believe me, Comrade Divisional Commander, it does happen.

You suddenly turned up at a lesson I was giving to one of the senior groups of radio telegraphists. You had an excellent knowledge of mathematics and of staff management; you were a fine, strict commander of the old, Tsarist army officer school. The rumour in college was that before the revolution you had shot your wife dead out of jealousy. If so, people like you fire at their wives only under extreme provocation.

When you suddenly came in to my lesson, for the first time in three years, I lost my head. After making a mess of delivering my report to you – and that was something you could not stand – I returned to the blackboard. You took a seat at the last desk at the back of the class.

The subject of my lecture was the division of inversely proportionate magnitudes. It's a rotten subject, Comrade Divisional Commander, and difficult to grasp even in outline. I always dealt with it in my own hand-to-mouth way but – honestly – my cadets understood me remarkably well. Your severe presence paralysed me. I should have been craftier and, instead of explaining the new subject, arranged a question-and-answer session, calling only the best cadets to the blackboard. But possibly because it was you, I did not want to resort to tricks.

As luck would have it, that very morning I had a splitting headache: I had been up half the night listening to the complaints of the battalion commander's wife about her husband. It was the usual kind of story in our officers' hostel. The battalion commander had married a waitress while he was still a platoon commander. He had spent three successive Saturdays courting her, with a weekend leave pass in his pocket, and on the fourth they signed the book at the Registry Office. He had immediately ordered her to give up her work. She had been glad to do so. Events then took their banal course. The platoon commander pursued his studies, further and additional rank insignia appeared on his collars, but his wife remained the ex-waitress. After dishing up breakfast for her husband, she would flop back into bed and sleep till midday. With hair all awry, in a soiled dressing gown, she would emerge to make her appearance in the kitchen. This was the common rendezvous of officers' wives in a position similar to hers. In our college, for some reason it was considered wrong for an officer's wife to work. It was somehow chic not to work.

They had their uniform – crêpe de Chine dress, lisle stockings and patent-leather shoes – in which they dressed up to attend the 1 May or 7 November parades. In essence these unfortunate women were deeply unhappy. The battalion commander's wife wept on my shoulder, repeating: "He has absolutely no respect for me."

I was the only bachelor in our entire, vastly long corridor. I was a point of refuge for hurt wives, and for husbands depressed by their consorts' appalling mediocrity.

By 4 a.m. I succeeded in coaxing the battalion commander from his room. He emerged half asleep, in his bare feet, a greatcoat over his underclothes.

Going up to his wife, he said: "Really, Tosya, what's the matter? That's enough. You should be ashamed of involving Comrade Teacher."

Tosya bawled even more loudly.

"I do your washing . . . I cook for you . . . You don't say a word to me, not a word."

"After all," said the battalion commander, "I get tired you know . . ." He turned round to me and said through his teeth: "To hell with her."

"Go up to her," I whispered.

He unwillingly took a pace nearer.

"Given in to your nerves, that's what you've done . . . I hand over my entire pay packet, to the last kopeck. Only take out enough to cover my Party fees and my smokes . . . You need a kid, Antonovna."

She buried her head in his chest: "Speak to me, Kostya dear."

The commander stole a look at his watch, over her shoulder.

"Very well," he sighed. "I'm not against it. Off we go, let's have a talk."

The next morning, after that sleepless night, you turned up at my class, Comrade Divisional Commander.

For forty-five minutes, with you watching, I squirmed before the blackboard, attempting to explain to the cadets the mysteries of the division of inversely proportionate magnitudes. They were sorry for me, and you noticed it.

Grey with rage, you sat there at the last desk at the back of the class. The following morning I was summoned to appear at staff headquarters.

"The diploma of graduation from a higher educational institution is missing from your papers."

I remained silent.

"Has it been mislaid?" the Commander asked.

"No," I said. "I never had one."

The Commander addressed me, without raising his head. Before him lay a thin file containing my personal records.

"Be so good as to explain on what basis you are doing teaching work?"

I was beyond caring. I replied: "On the basis of my love for it."

He gave me a quick glance.

"You ought to go on trial for misrepresentation. You are making illegal use of the title of pedagogue. Instead of entering an institute at the appropriate moment and obtaining a diploma . . ."

"Comrade Chief of Staff," I said, "I applied four times for admission at the appropriate moment. I'm listed as a fifth-category citizen, the son of a private tradesman." He said nothing for quite a while. I even wondered whether he had forgotten about me.

Tiring of standing at attention, I shuffled from foot to foot, examining the walls of the ascetically sparse office.

"In your Labour Book," the Commander's voice penetrated my hearing, "there are a number of favourable entries. They are, I assume, genuine?"

I nodded.

He was now looking at me fixedly, not at my face, but lower down, at my chest. And his gaze was an absent-minded, thoughtful one, as if through me he saw something else on which he was called to pass judgement.

"I am dismissing you," the Commander finally said.

On my way to the door I heard his exasperated voice: "Your dismissal will be recorded as due to staff cuts."

In fact, you were right, Alexander Vasilevich. And thank you for not putting something prejudicial in my Labour Book. To use the terminology of natural science, I am embarking on a molecular analysis of our life. If one analyses it at the organic level, it emerges that for many long years we have shown very little difference from one another. This presented the option of examining us on the basis of an average. So as to simplify the process, we started to be called "cadres". At times the terminology conformed to the principle: it derived from the principle.

Cadres decide everything, Stalin said. He could not have proceeded on the basis of the formula "people decide everything", because for him the notion "people" was superfluous and even hampering. People – in actual fact – could decide everything: as regards cadres, they are mutually replaceable – you have to count their numbers but you do not have to take them into account.

In my view, never was there such a mass need to come to terms with our past as that which is now generally evident. Our past is a mystery. It is a mystery not so much in terms of the facts, which in due course will come to light again and again, as in terms of its psychology.

That is exactly how I see it. I have enough facts. I have a bellyful of them.

I am suffering from methodological undernourishment.

Facts cannot explain what I find to be the most important thing – people's psychology.

In our exploration of the past, of its recesses, each of us stops short at a point beyond which he is unable to explore; for young people, things are easier – they travel light, free from the burden of complicity. I am not speaking of criminal complicity. My molecular analysis permits me to scrutinize even thought complicity. "This happened while I was there and I agreed with it" – that is what I have in mind. And that is the point at which one slows down the pace, at which we stray back into the framework of our own life. On arrival at this point we take up positions of all-round defence and fight to the penultimate bullet, because the last one we keep for ourselves.

For me this point is Lenin. The revolution and the beginning of the twenties.

And the more furious the defensive fire I lay down from this vantage point, the more mysterious I find the sequel to those events.

Primitive man's faith in God has been built up over thousands of years. It has been passed on from generation to generation. The hypocrisy of religion has been a relative hypocrisy – it did not promise a heaven on earth. It told fibs about the gardens of Paradise. The notion of God was speculative. Or rather it became increasingly a matter for speculation as mankind developed in cultural terms.

And suddenly God turned out to be a close neighbour. He materialized in the one country that had become almost totally anti-religious. This god was very much a concrete god. He went around in brilliantly polished high jackboots, in a trench coat, and in a peaked cap of a semi-military cut. Icons bearing his likeness were printed by the million.

Even the tenants of communal flats turned their premises into prayer houses.

Community meetings started to resemble flagellants' sessions of penance.

Sectarians started scourging themselves before the eyes of the true believers.

This God was a merciless god. He administered retribution not in the next world but in this. And the more punishment he dealt out, the more ecstatically people believed in him. Not one of the apostles betrayed him: he ended up betraying all of them.

From the origins of Christianity to the time when millions of people came to believe in Christ, centuries elapsed. The new god emerged after Lenin's death and, in the course of fifteen to seventeen years, a naïve, blind faith in him overcame hundreds of millions of people.

The printers ran out of type for the daily commemoration

of his name. He was omniscient – he was designated "the Coryphæus of Science". His concurrence was required for deciding on the wing profile of aeroplanes, wheat mutations, the mechanical efficiency of railway locomotives, questions of linguistics, exact time schedules for splitting the atom; for pronouncing on the subject matter of films, or questions of history, of philosophy, of literature . . .

He was all-seeing and all-hearing – through the eyes and ears of his informers. From being a secret, ignoble occupation, denunciation became an honourable civic duty.

He was all-powerful and omnipresent – his archangels prised people out of their warm beds at night, removed them from trains, picked them up in the street, awaited them in the theatres with orders for their arrest.

For such behaviour Emperors, the Lord's Anointed, earned themselves hatred; they were strangled, shot, and deposed.

The new god was worshipped.

His praises were extolled in songs and anthems; he was cast in bronze, sculpted in marble, portrayed in oils, depicted on stage and on the screen. His name was conferred on cities and villages.

His works were studied in day nurseries, kindergartens, schools and universities.

Starving people thanked him for their full stomachs. Those facing death at his hand shouted out hosannas in his honour.

I was a witness to this.

I cannot understand this.

Attempts to explain this mystery of human psychology in terms of ever-present fear are unfounded. Fear and only fear would not be capable of reducing a two-hundred-million-strong population over the course of thirty years to a state of permanent genuflection.

There is another explanation. It does not seem to me exhaustive.

They say he was the exponent and executant of the idea the realization of which is mankind's age-long dream. And that we focused on him our love for this dream.

Maybe at first this was how it was. But within only a few years the result of his actions was in cruel contrast with this idea, abusing it and drowning it in grief and blood. The disparity between word and deed was visible to a child but passed unperceived by intelligent adults. Or else they were aware of it but said that that was how things had to be.

One cannot ask History the question: what would have happened if . . . ? For History this question is ruled out. History is always determinist. What happened, happened – that is the only line of reasoning it knows.

I want no part of this determinism.

I want to know what would have happened if it had not happened.

And what will happen.

After my dismissal from the military college, I soon found another job. The Communications Institute took me on as a teacher in its SSF – Special Services Faculty.

There was nothing mysterious behind these, to us Russians, apparently secretive initials: the SSF taught heads of post offices, of telegraph offices and head people on the communications side in general.

[121]

In terms of preparation, these students were little different from those at my Communist University. Except, maybe, in knowing the communications business and having a specific profession.

The SSF had a profile of its own: each faculty group numbered no more than three or four students. In some cases, the entire group consisted of a single student. He was a valuable property and had as many teachers assigned to him personally as would be assigned to a normal student group.

In those years this system of instruction was followed not only in our Communications Institute. It was widespread. The need for it arose because management found it increasingly difficult to discharge their responsibilities without some modicum of knowledge: the level of knowledge of those under them was rising year by year and, for that matter, the operational side was getting more complex.

Work at the SSF was boring – it smacked of repetitive coaching. The teachers' efforts, compressed, as it were, inside a tube, were squirted onto each student like so much toothpaste. My SSF students studied without any particular keenness: all they needed was their leaving certificate.

There were not enough lecture rooms. Often the students would come around to my flat. Our relations thus became semi-domestic. It was, in practice, difficult to award a guest a gamma mark within the confines of your own room – you felt awkward in doing so. Then, too, I gradually came to the conclusion that these students did not need my rudimentary mathematics.

I became an uncaring teacher.

I became increasingly dissatisfied.

The years were going by. The excitement of teaching and acquiring knowledge was palling on me and I was becoming a cold technician.

My life was not working out. It proceeded, as it were, on two non-interlocking planes. In both it suffered from deformity: I was a pseudo-teacher and I had no place of my own in this world. A feeling of impermanency in what I was doing and how I was living increasingly took over.

. . . It's quite true, Zinaida Borisovna – from time to time I did try my hand at literary scribbling.

Sasha wrote poetry, did you know that? At that time almost all my friends composed verse. Perhaps it was the effect those days had on us? I didn't have that particular urge. When I felt the need to express myself in poetry, I recited other people's verse – and that more than sufficed. In declaiming it out loud I sort of migrated into the poem and was proud of living in it, of finding such a splendid way of saying what I wanted to say.

Our attitude toward poetry then was different from what it is now. I did not expect or demand of the poems that they should explain my surroundings to me. I even fell in love with imperfectly understood poems. The recitation of poetry excited me like sorcery, like black magic.

I do not remember our dividing poetry into lyric and civic. Into courageous and cowardly. My friends and I had no need for the virtues of the new Socialist regime to be propagated in verse. And there was no need for the regime to be defended from us. In all probability, the need we felt was for the poems – assuming they were supposed to explain anything at all – to explain us to ourselves.

We were good readers. It never occurred to us that we might tell a poet what he should write about. For me a good poet was, and still is, a magician. What rare herbs go into the making of his poetry is a mystery to me, and if I were to discover it, the magic would be lost.

The muffled echoes of battle between the literary trends did reach my ears, but the incoherent medley of their rallying cries made no impression on me. I loved poets, even those who were at loggerheads. Much later I was to learn about their theoretical platforms but, as a rule, those platforms merely detracted from my adoration for my idols. I believe that the reader is always bound to feel deceived on getting to know his beloved poet personally. Poetic masterpieces are always better, purer and more stunning than their master, for the poetry gives expression to the ultimate heights of his genius.

Do I have the right to say so, Zinaida Borisovna?

Your letters about Sasha happen to have set off a mechanism inside me which is now ticking away, irrespective of what I want. I have lost control over it. The past is moving around inside me like a tracer element on no set course. It should therefore be supremely easy for me to record the events of my life. So why is it that I find writing so difficult?

Literature did not become my profession. I am an amateur. My scribbling came about by chance.

When I was living in Dudergof, to the southwest of Leningrad, in camp, teaching the military cadets mathematics, I got desperately bored in the evenings. One was not allowed into town. So, perhaps from boredom, I wrote something. It was published, but this in no way changed my long-term intentions. Teaching attracted me as before, although I continued to feel less and less secure in the profession. Literary vanity did not put down any deep roots in me – I had written myself out in my very first manuscript. And my life seemed to lose direction: having not become a littérateur, I was gradually ceasing to be a teacher.

As is always the case, I now understand this much more fully and better than I did then. The disquiet which then overcame me had only one result – my longing for Katya became even greater.

"We have discussed the matter," the Institute Director said, "and decided that the vacated room in Sipovsky's flat can be allocated to you."

I was still living in the officers' hostel, from which feeble but persistent efforts were being made to evict me.

"Here's a possession order," said the Director, avoiding my gaze. "You should move in as soon as possible. Your furniture is presumably government issue?"

I nodded.

"Buy yourself a stool or a chair, get your things together, and move in tomorrow. Secure the door with a padlock. Do you have a padlock?"

I asked: "But does Grigory Mitrofanovich's wife know that you are providing me with a possession order?"

"She doesn't know. And is not to know. Until the minute you take your things into the vacated room. Otherwise there'll be a muddle and the Institute will lose the room. I had to fight tooth and nail for it with the local authorities."

"I don't feel like . . ." I started.

"Don't feel like – then don't take it," said the Director. "The next on the list of those acutely in need of housing is Alekseev, the fireman. He's a regular attendant at the dispensary. He has serious drinking bouts three times a year. He'll reduce the entire flat to a shambles."

I phoned Grigory Mitrofanovich's wife that same evening. We hardly knew him – he worked in the Political Economy faculty – and his wife not at all. I recounted to her my conversation with the Director and advised her to go to a legal aid centre and try to secure the return of her husband's office, at least up to such time as sentence was passed on him.

"The order is valid for a month," I said. "If nothing works out, please let me know what you decide."

Three days later I received an urban telegram: BEG YOU TO MOVE IN. I transferred myself to what had been Sipovsky's office, without bothering to buy either stool or chair. There was no chance of my accustoming myself to living in an arrested man's flat. It was the second time it happened to me somehow to do a person a favour by interfering with the normal course of their life.

I was not to live for long in the flat with Evgenia Markovna. Two months or so after my moving in she received a summons from the local militia station – and this boded ill.

I went along with her. She was in a bad way.

I waited for Evgenia Markovna in the little square with the statue of Lomonosov, next to the militia station, with her one-year-old daughter on my knees. I didn't have very long to wait – I learned subsequently that Evgenia Markovna had been taken ill in the militia chief's office. She had been given a drink of water to bring her round as well as a written order to leave Leningrad for Kazakhstan within three days.

The following two days were spent selling off the furniture for a pittance. The second-hand shops were full to bursting with the possessions of people who had suffered repression. Cupboards, grand pianos, sideboards were all dragged down the stairs or hauled laboriously out through the window frames on straps.

In a now empty room, all dusty and begrimed from the boots of the furniture porters, and bearing the scars of the photographs ripped down from the walls, I said goodbye to Evgenia Markovna.

There was a draught blowing in from the open doors and windows.

I no longer remember whether it was autumn or not.

It was in the year of grace 1938.

My new flat-sharer was Kesha Valdaev. His proper Christian names were, I think, Innokenty Ivanovich. We were the same age and were soon on intimate terms.

Kesha served in the NKVD in some sort of guard unit. Just who he guarded from whom I never found out exactly, and I didn't pursue the point, although on my rare visits to the theatre, I would sometimes come across Kesha in the foyer: over six feet in height and broad in the shoulders, with an anxious look on his face, he would be bodily easing the interval strollers out of the path of someone unseen by me who had just emerged from the government box.

He died just five years ago, did Kesha. Long before his death, he had been demobilized with the rank of major in the KGB. My recent meetings with him had become fewer. He seemed to me not a bad chap. The son of a cook, a factory lathe operator in the past who had got into the NKVD as the result of a trawl among the Komsomol, he had never been an investigator nor a special operative – his height and size immediately singled him out for guard service at the Smolny Party Headquarters.

There was something caring about Kesha. He was capable of registering astonishment, even then, in those years. I don't know to what I owed Kesha's trust in me but even when we were living at different ends of the city, he would send me complimentary seats for the public stands by the Winter Palace on the eve of the two major parades.

I used to visit him. Apart from me, the others sitting at the long, abundantly laden table were all Kesha's fellow officials. Looking at them, I felt such blood-curdling interest that I could not taste the food. By then I had no illusions about the character of their work. I used to discuss trivialities with them, listen to their jokes, dance with their wives, but my sole head-splitting thought while doing so was: What about yesterday, and tomorrow morning? What were you doing yesterday, and what will you be up to tomorrow morning . . . ?

Late one night Kesha and I went out to get some fresh air into our muzzy heads. He may have been a shade more drunk than I. Even by the light of the streetlamp, I could see how pale his face looked.

I asked: "Tired, Kesha?"

"One does get tired," he said.

We were standing on the embankment. The public holiday had ended the previous day, but various illuminations were still twinkling. At that hour there were no passers-by.

Kesha suddenly slammed his vast fist against the granite parapet. And, stranger still, gave a broad smile.

"What a job! Five hours' sleep in three whole days, not more. And d'you know why? Looking for bombs, infernal machines . . ."

"Which ones?" I hadn't understood him.

"Devil only knows! . . . I spend my whole time looking. In twelve years, I've never found a damned thing."

"Do you need to?" I asked.

"And how!" Kesha scowled. "Factories have their plans, and so do we."

I held my tongue, expecting him to take fright the very next second at what he had just said to me.

But he didn't.

"Can you explain to me," said Kesha, bringing his fixed smile right up to me, "what in the hell our organs need a plan for? What is there to plan?"

The question was not addressed to me. I did not have to supply an answer.

It was a long time before we met again. I heard from somewhere that Kesha had been pensioned off. At his age he could have served longer, but it was evidently a case of the latest contingent of long-serving officials being eased out.

We met for the last time in '56. And quarrelled.

Kesha came to see me with a request. His son was preparing for entry into an institute: a fortnight or so before the exams he needed extra coaching in the curriculum. We settled that point straightaway. However, in the expectation that Kesha

[129]

was happy at the news of the past twelve months, I said: "How good it is, old friend, that we have lived to see these days! Thank God, at last we have heard the truth."

He looked at me scornfully: "What's good about it? We've shot our mouth off for the whole world to hear."

"But it's the truth. You after all, Kesha, know what a terrible truth it was."

"So what? I do know. But there's no point in clacking about it. Who's the better off for it, this truth? D'you think it'll make people believe more? We've simply covered ourselves with shit in front of the whole world."

I became indignant.

"In other words, you think we should have left innocent people to rot in the prisons and camps?"

"Why so? It should have been done on the quiet. Without the claptrap. They went in on the quiet. They should have been let out on the quiet."

"But what about those who died?"

"Will they come back to life because of it?" – Kesha sighed deeply and genuinely. "They've put all the blame on the lads from the organs. There were monstrosities, that I know. But the overall result is discreditation."

By then I had already had occasion to hear arguments along those lines, so I looked at Kesha with bored ferocity. He evidently sensed this. His already flushed face – he had high blood pressure – now became menacingly grey: "Just how do you see it? Tell me – the investigator lifted his little finger and the prison door opened – was that it? If he felt like it, he gave him one in the kisser? . . . He's just a pawn, the investigator, you know! Less than a worm. He has his orders: he carries them out. If you had served, you'd have done the same."

"I didn't serve," I said.

"But others did," said Kesha. "Do you have anything to drink?"

I poured him half a tumbler of vodka, and myself too, but I didn't touch it, though it escaped his notice.

"There was more discipline," said Kesha. "People need authority. Firm authority. To feel a strong hand. Our country lad has to feel it. And factory hands too."

"And you?" I asked.

"Me what?"

"Do you need it?"

"I too need it. There are people who have better brains than us. That's their line of business – to think out government policy. Let's have a drop more vodka."

I pushed my still half-full tumbler across to him. I wanted him to leave there and then. Certain irreversible changes had taken place in him. Previously he never became drunk from vodka, but simply seized up. Now, however, his movements had become tentative, his eyes, deadened by alcohol, had lost all sparkle.

I asked: "Kesha, did you beat anyone up?"

"Now, now . . ." Kesha said, and threatened me with his finger.

We quarrelled just before his departure. As we were saying goodbye in the entrance lobby, he gave me a hug: "Thank you about my Vova. Just have a word with the institute director or someone. Crafty like, in your Jewish way . . ."

"Wha-at?" I broke in on him.

"Well, what's so wrong about that?" Kesha smiled artlessly. "Your nation sticks together, not like we Russian fools. You always look after one another . . ."

I pushed him to one side, opened the door, and, ashamed for him, for the people responsible for crippling him, for the time in which I was living, forcibly ejected Kesha from the house.

All of a sudden things took a sharp turn for the better for Igor Astakhov. It emerged that with a dab of make-up he could easily be turned into Stalin.

The theatre in which he was working put on some historic play in which Igor came out onto the stage smoking a pipe, his hair cut short, and wearing a trench coat: the audience gave him ovation after ovation. He was one of the first actors to learn how to play this role. And such was the magical power of the role that its charisma, even off the stage, outside the play, somehow continued to shed its aura on the theatrical troupe. The mere fact that that particular trench coat was constantly draped on a coat hanger in Astakhov's dressing room, that a certain semi-military-style peaked cap was to be seen on his shelf and a particular pair of high-heeled leather boots on his floor – this alone was enough to compel the theatre management to reassess their attitude toward Igor.

He became a top-category actor.

It was not possible to say of him that he played the part badly, since his outward resemblance to Stalin gave him total immunity.

The few remarks which Astakhov uttered from the stage with a barely discernible Georgian accent, the few poses –

familiar from portraits and news film – which he struck during the show, transported him to another plane where the air was rarer, where the spectator found breathing difficult and rewarding.

Astakhov's reception in Moscow was even more tumultuous. He was asked to appear in a film.

He no longer played any other parts: the directors were afraid that he might spoil his key role by investing it with common mannerisms.

I found it increasingly difficult to go and see them. My relations with Katya had come to a halt, and had done so at a point from which they could move only in a backward direction. After what had happened in Batiliman, Astakhov's benevolence had become strained. It was not enmity for one another that we felt, but mutual inadequacy. Katya took from each of us what she prized and what she needed, and from these contributions she made up a single person for herself, so that now Igor and I had no existence as individuals.

Even so, it was easier for him. I was on my way home: he had her staying with him.

Very occasionally I used to have a burning urge to get my revenge for my disinheritance. But whenever I felt that way, things became still worse. Each would-be act of vengeance tended to demean me still further.

I can now judge it all from afar. I could well refashion my entire life from beginning to end, but the one part I would not touch is Katya. Neither the pain, nor the ecstasy. I would not forswear even the self-contempt which at times took possession of me. Nor the pitiful place I occupied alongside her.

[133]

As Pushkin has said, may the Lord grant you the love of another such.

Their life underwent a startling change. First there appeared a fine flat in Leningrad. Then a car of their own. They started to number among their guests people who were household names. I circulated diffidently among them. Sometimes I interrupted their looks of puzzlement, but these people did not allow themselves to waste their attention on me.

It was difficult for me.

I was the odd man out.

Not merely because I was poorer than them. Or because I could not follow what they were talking about. I was unable to relate to their way of thinking. These arts personalities were already pirouetting in that dust-laden vortex of shameless success and personal wellbeing through which they failed to perceive life's actualities.

They were still not cynics. They were still under the impression of not actually lying. They were charged with the task of portraying a make-believe life, and even when they started to realize that it was make-believe, they rearranged themselves back into a state of sincere belief, for they assumed that there were higher postulates requiring them to behave thus. But those who laid down these postulates, on seeing how readily and urgently all this was performed, first rewarded the performers but then demanded of them still greater dissimulation.

A new breed of men emerged – the well-paid fanatics. This breed of fanaticism is particularly dangerous. They stop at nothing – they have much to lose. Their defences are drawn up in considerable depth: they have hypocrisy and cynicism lined up in support.

Igor Astakhov was also sucked into this vortex: he cavorted with his false friends in good fortune, but his innate inconsequentiality kept him from occupying any position of consequence. He was simply and unthinkingly happy.

The sudden cascade of material privilege that descended on him did not change his character. I have the impression that he did not believe in his talent. Astakhov considered that he had been fortunate and that it was up to him to make the best of his good fortune. He squeezed the maximum that could be obtained from his position but knew when to stop short if he saw he was going too far.

Katya was more intelligent than him.

She wanted more for Astakhov. While luxuriating in the largesse that came their way she saw it as something fortuitous. What she dreamed of was a reward that they had earned as their right.

As with many women, all her vanity was centred on the man with whom she lived. Astakhov's work in the theatre and the cinema seemed to her to be of insufficient value. For that very reason she sought desperately to persuade herself and those around her that such work required special talent.

I dislike that period of Katya's life. I dislike recalling it and I disliked it at the time. Many of us plumbed the depths in those years. For some they were deeper, for others they were shallower. Some lived comfortably, others experienced hardship.

The Astakhovs had taken up residence in Moscow.

We saw one another seldom, and the distance between us

grew. I made one further attempt – the last one, this time – to break free. However strange it may seem, the mistakes to which one is most prone are one's old mistakes.

I had found living alone unbearable. I had to have someone to hurry home to, someone to whom I could say what it was I liked and what it was I detested. I needed someone to take care of. Inexhaustible supplies of solicitude bequeathed to me by my father were fermenting in my veins. I persuaded myself that I could manage to do this, even without love. I considered that one could start from that stage of married life at which one normally only arrives when one has got to the end of the course.

I proposed to the English-language teacher Vera Mikhailovna Kruglova. In the literal sense, I put the proposal to her. I said: "Marry me."

We were on our way home from the Institute and when we reached the tram stop outside the Kazan Cathedral I had the phrase pat. There was almost no preface, apart from something about my loneliness.

Vera Mikhailovna already had her foot on the lower step of the tram. Waving goodbye, she said: "Mind you – I may perhaps not agree."

We often walked as far as that stop. It was here she took a No. 12 tram to where she lived on Staro-Nevsky Street. And I turned off down the Griboedov Canal. In the Institute we only saw one another in the breaks. If one totted up our entire time together over the year, it would have amounted to no more than a few days. Yet people would say, they've known each other for a whole year.

I was not mistaken in Vera Mikhailovna. What attracted me

about her still held good after we came together. I was mistaken in myself.

The calm and assurance that she gave off acted on me like a sedative. I had been tearing myself apart from the tension that had taken possession of me in the Astakhov household, the need to keep up with Katya, to justify what she thought she saw in me – I was nothing but nerve ends. Here I could be myself. Or so it seemed to me.

We joined forces. The life I had logically projected began. It was a marriage put together in the laboratory. Everything about it had its set place. The two elements of which it was composed entered into contact. Two no longer young individuals – I was getting on for thirty and Vera Mikhailovna was five years older – with distinct experiences and distinctly formed characters, with no memories in common, with passion left out of the equation, started getting to know one another by "letting events take their turn," i.e., by trial and error. The working mechanism was set in motion with its parts showing signs of wear, without even having been properly run in. And they had been assembled by a bungler.

Vera Mikhailovna said, when presenting me to her friends: "Meet my spouse."

I gave a shudder – the word was not in my vocabulary.

We tried very hard to please one another. I read to her while she was embroidering. And I hated reading out loud. She liked it. So I fell in line.

When I awoke in the middle of the night I would sense with the entire right-hand side of my body that someone alien to me was lying beside me. Even Valya Snegiryova was closer to me than that – we did have the citadel of youth in common.

[137]

That summer, during the vacations, I took Vera Mikhailovna to Kharkov to see my parents.

My mother had by now learned patience: three sons had already escorted seven fiancées along to see her. This had taught her to be evasive. There were times when she would say, sadly: "I'm going a bit giddy from all these young ladies."

She greeted Vera Mikhailovna with her usual cordiality, plus a measure of well-concealed curiosity.

We spent ten days or so in Kharkov. I introduced my new wife to my surviving childhood friends – Tosik Zunin and Misha Sinkov had already disappeared without trace.

We paid a visit to Sasha Belyavsky.

The once majestic Great Dane, Rex, lay on its couch, semi-paralysed. It tried to get up to greet us but could only raise its front quarters, surmounted by a heavy, bony head. After a friendly quiver to us, it lay down again.

Everything in Sasha's house had grown mangy and neglected: the two carpets, one on the wall, one on the floor, the yellowing ivory paper-knife, the mirrors dulled over. Time had affected everything save Sergey Pavlovich. He was as provincially elegant and fragrant as ever. I very much wanted Vera Mikhailovna to feel at home in this house, in this part of my past. I sensed that she was not coming to terms with my past. In essence, I knew nothing about her. What she said about herself did not give me an overall picture – it was all impersonal and disembodied.

Only fragmentary memories remain of that visit to Sasha's house: the look of studied refinement on Vera Mikhailovna's face as she listened to Sasha reading poetry, the hoarse sound of his guttural voice, and snatches of my conversation with him: "What's become of Tosik and Misha?"

"No change," said Sasha.

"Any idea of what they're accused of?"

"They're said to be accused of taking part in some organization or other."

"Can you see them doing that?"

"A matter of imagination," said Sasha.

Our talk was brief. We were probably already frightened of one another. Both he and I believed in the innocence of our childhood friends, but we ourselves – friends from childhood – no longer believed in one another.

This abominable distrust that makes you repulsive to your own self was absorbed into the bloodstream and part of the very air we breathed. People continued to exist normally with poison that would have driven an animal mad in their system.

While earnestly suspecting a friend of betrayal, they drank vodka with him; teachers were scared stiff of their pupils; and their pupils of them. Terrified of being denounced and detesting denunciation, people made haste to get in first with the denouncing so as to be ahead of the pack.

I am not speaking of that sick madness that was extorted from people under torture. Nor of anonymous letters, whether sent off unsigned or under a pseudonym. I am speaking of that open and infectious form of denunciation which became a genre of its own in literature and art, a separate branch of science, a device in the practice of public speaking.

The denunciations came out in print in the form of poetry or prose, as paintings from someone's brush, as graphic art from someone's atelier, and left their imprint on music too.

Denunciations masquerading as films taught children to keep a vigilant eye on their own parents. In their postgraduate and doctoral dissertations academics denounced their colleagues. It was not individuals who were targeted but map references, entire branches of science marked down for total destruction by the napalm effect of calumny.

The tale bearers advanced openly to take their stand at the rostrum, their heads raised high, their faces glowing with rage. There was no longer any need to hire their services. In their eagerness to get to the rostrum they elbowed each other aside. They burnished the art of denunciation to the gleam of a finely honed knife and plunged it into their victim's spine – not his chest. Before our eyes they cut the throats of our friends with this blade.

We had no right to shed tears. We had no right to look on in frozen silence. We were required to applaud. The virus of suspicion of one another ate into our brains, irradiated our genes, changing their code – it became hereditary.

And amid all this people worked. Worked hard, oblivious of self or of their own advantage. Risked their lives for the sake of the happiness of mankind. Like a mirage, this happiness receded further and further into the distance. People kept advancing toward it like ants, overburdened, indefatigable: on meeting fallen comrades in their path, they would crawl past them and continue dragging their burden ahead.

The period showed that man does not know the limits of his potential – whether for heroism or for ignominy.

I find chronology a nuisance: it gets in one's way. Seeking to impose a logical sequence that would only be cumbersome.

In a man's life there are events firmly affixed to a certain date and time. But there are others for which the year, the month and the day become immaterial: they are transcendental happenings.

Katya left Igor Astakhov and came to join me. This occurrence repeated itself often enough later, but that was the first occasion.

The train came late at night.

I saw her on the other side of the train window as it crawled along the platform.

She scrabbled at the glass and gave me a smile and I walked alongside.

She had not that much luggage – just two suitcases. I always looked to see how much she was carrying, the moment she appeared at the head of the carriage steps: I learned to tell from the number of suitcases how long she was leaving Astakhov for.

That first time we went from the station to a hotel. We had nowhere to stay. My flat was occupied by my wife, Vera Mikhailovna.

I had become completely entangled. Or rather I had never disentangled myself. Neither Katya nor I was a free person in the ordering of our lives. I didn't have the strength to turn down what came my way. I wanted more, but without even that pittance I would have ceased to mean anything to myself. I would have ceased to exist.

Our route from the station took us along the Nevsky Prospect.

I had no flat to offer Katya, but I did have this empty city awaking with the dawn – I set great store by it.

The four horses I had installed on Anichkov Bridge turned

their long, kindly muzzles toward us. Those familiar naked boys were trying to hold them back. The horses were wrestling free from the boys' grip in order to come to Katya.

As the Nevsky was empty, I had populated it with the help of my unsystematized imagination. There were the two great captains – Kutuzov and Barclay de Tolly – waiting to greet us at the Kazan Cathedral, their bronze swords at the salute. In front of the Astoria there was Nicholas I on his prancing steed.

We took the cheapest room available, using Katya's Moscow passport. Its windows gave onto an inner courtyard which ended in a blank wall.

And yet again time ceased to count and all thoughts save the single mad one flew out of my head – that of pinning down this meaningless moment of existence. The incompleteness of the happiness which I had to measure in moments made me lose my bearings. Unable to believe that it would continue, I dropped everything in order to secure its continuation. The world around me lost its proportions. I had to strip away everything that was not essential in terms of now, or today, or this very minute. My hearing, my field of vision knew but one recognizable object – Katya.

The money soon gave out – both mine and Katya's. I had a lot of books. I had been collecting books for some fifteen years. After selling them off to the second-hand bookshops, we left for the south.

In the right-hand pigeonhole of my writing desk there were for a long time letters written in her hand. They continued arriving after we had separated. The last letter from her I received at the end of the war. My neighbour from the next-door flat on our landing, who had only survived the siege by a miracle, handed it to me in 1945. I did not even begin to read it. It was dead. It was alien, as though written not to me and not by Katya. Two strangers, unknown to me, had been exchanging letters and I had no right to pry into their relationship.

Every four months or so in the course of tidying up my desk I would come across these unopened envelopes. They kept needling me like shell fragments concealed behind scar tissue. There was no pain, but the joints had lost their flexibility in that area and seemed unable to bend at the point where they met.

And so, in 1949, when Katya was arrested, I burned them all, still unread.

I burned them out of cowardice.

There was no logic in what I did. The wave of postwar repression knocked me off balance. The howls set up by the press and radio, the hysterical calls emanating from public meetings, drove me into a beat demarcated by flags. The marksmen, posted at their numbered hides, with one ear to the cries of the beaters, fired into the crowd, without taking aim, going just by the sound. We kept closing ranks, filling the gaps and waiting for the noise of the next fusillade.

It turned out that one could get used to it.

The theatres continued working, the famous musicians and pianists continued playing with the symphony orchestras, gigantic new blast furnaces were brought into operation, vast dams of unprecedented dimensions constructed, weddings celebrated, children born in the same time-honoured way, and the sun continued rising and setting. Everything went on as if nothing had happened.

It was only night that brought bad dreams.

*   *   *

I first spotted him on our dusty village square. He wore an oldish, sun-faded gown flung, evidently, over his underpants and a T-shirt – the grey hairs of his chest protruded from the unbuttoned neck of his gown. A capacious basket lay at his feet and these were accommodated in domestic flip-flops. The basket held a selection of fresh root vegetables, each portion done up in newspaper – spring onions, sticks of young celery, fennel.

The spot he had chosen to ply his modest trade was a well-frequented one: the regular bus service went past it and the stop was not far away.

In those days we had no bazaar in our village: the solitary salesman helped provide the weekenders with fresh vegetables. The prices he asked were reasonable.

I myself sometimes bought his produce. It is hard to stand in the sun by the dusty roadside – I felt sorry for this elderly man. The thing that astounded me was that he had chosen a rather exposed place: on the other side of the square stood the two-storey headquarters of the local militia. The youthful militiamen, brought up with the idea that private trade is a breeding ground for capitalist sharks, glanced at him with a scowl. However – and this was the odd thing – they never moved him on. Sometimes he was approached by the station head, First Lieutenant Tomilin, who would request him plaintively: "Can't you at least put some trousers on, Comrade Colonel?"

The huckster would twitch his gown back into place and reply politely: "It's hot, Tomilin."

"Aren't you ashamed to be seen like that?" Tomilin asked. "You draw a pension, you've got money from your official awards . . . Yet here you are, trading on the street, in broad daylight in a village centre."

Removing his reddish-brown velour hat and exposing a moist stark-white bald pate, the huckster said: "Why do you have to pick on me, Tomilin? I'm only selling my own produce. You won't get at me that way. You should read the papers. The consumer is the thing. And the consumer needs soup. And soup needs root vegetables. I am making up for the underperformance of the State trading network."

"You've no conscience," said the militia inspector.

"You've slipped up again. Don't you know the latest guidelines? Conscience is a notion outside Party terms of reference – it can be ours but it can sometimes not be ours."

The well-read colonel had no difficulty in getting the best of the ignorant first lieutenant.

I was a frequent witness to these lackadaisical ideological encounters. I tended toward an attitude of squeamish sympathy with the kerbside dealer in root vegetables. Since I was unaware of the circumstances of his life, I was not going to risk condemning him. All the more so because in our village there was no other way of obtaining root vegetables for making soup.

My final attitude to him was determined by chance, in the course of a fishing expedition.

[145]

We met on the lake, near White Cottages – the name given to a cluster of light-coloured buildings extending along the high shore of this vast lake. I knew that for some time – for the past fifteen years or so – this was a place where retired people had been living.

Our two boats were close to one another. There were not many fish in the lake. After they had been frequently stunned with dynamite or poisoned with lime, there were only the small fry which, by the grace of God, survived to flutter through the reservoir. But even they were difficult to capture with hook and line.

The evening sunset was already over; the sun had gone in but the incandescent sky had yet to cool down.

I settled down close to a small, bare little island, fouled by gulls' droppings. This bird, romantic in flight, is highly slovenly in its actual habits. The entire expanse of pebbles along the foreshore and all the rocks on the island itself were coated with the gulls' excrement.

When I clambered ashore and lit a small bonfire with the aid of lengths of dry reed, the birds hovered over my head, shrieking at me in their raucous, guttersnipe voices: their gawky, misshapen fledglings, covered with fur rather than feathers, strutted between the rocks.

I had it in mind to stay there for the night, right up to dawn.

I could already hear the creaking of oars in the rowlocks – another boat was coming inshore.

The old-age pensioner emerged from the dusk in answer to my bonfire. He was now trimly dressed in a padded jacket and high gumboots.

[146]

"Any objection?"

He sat down on a stone on the other side of the fire.

We exchanged a few remarks about the fishing, and then I asked: "What branch of the services were you in, Comrade Colonel?"

After a moment's silence, he replied: "In the organs."

"For long?"

"Since 1930. Celebrated my twenty-five years with them in 1955. Took my pension early for health reasons."

"What's wrong with your health?" I asked.

"Liver," said the colonel. "Heart. Central nervous system. We have the complete range of invalids in White Cottages." He looked at me through the flames of the bonfire and, presumably failing to detect my expression, added: "Insomnia is the very devil."

"What's the problem?" I said.

"You get off for an hour and then toss about till the early hours. A matter of age. You probably have the same problem?"

"No," I said. "My medical history is a different one." We were the same generation. But I did not want to have even insomnia in common with him.

"You're not a doctor, by any chance?" asked the colonel.

I shook my head.

"Our medicine's fallen behind," sighed the colonel. "When it's a matter of lopping off arms or legs, we're fine, but when it comes to sewing up nerve endings, we haven't a clue. Abroad, it's said, they do it with pills. And the way they treat you there, it's a bloody miracle. Not like our ham-fisted sawbones."

[147]

"Article 58, section 10," I said. "In '49 you were putting people behind bars for saying things like that."

He raised his face and gave me a cool look.

"It depends on the concrete historical situation."

"So you don't blame yourself for anything?"

"Personally, you mean?"

"If you wish."

"There were times when I made mistakes, but the general line was correct." He grabbed one of the fledglings lying on the far side of a rock. "I'm fed up to the teeth with these questions."

"Mere children," I said, "small children were taken away from their arrested parents and handed over to an orphanage under a number. And newly born babies were put in prison along with their mothers."

"How wise everyone's now become." The colonel suppressed a yawn. "Talk their heads off, they do. What's your profession?"

"I'm a teacher."

"What did you teach the school kids? To stand up for the Soviet regime? Well, I too stood up for it. I spent twenty years standing up and protecting its ideas. If I had done my work badly I wouldn't have been allowed to retire honourably. The government has accorded me my just deserts, but from people in the street I get nothing but reproach." He put the fledgling back in exactly the same place, then went off and relieved himself. On returning, he said: "I've had more than enough of such talk. You take a seat in one of the suburban trains and every tin-pot intellectual thinks he has a licence to hold forth. They've done everything possible to please him: publicly

[148]

admitted to the infringements, restored Socialist justice and Socialist norms. OK, so now get down to it, start working, studying, building a new society. But that's not enough for the little sniveller. He turns his nose up. Sings anti-Soviet songs to the sound of his guitar . . . If I had my way . . ."

I asked: "You'd put them behind bars?"

"Why so? There's no guideline to that effect now. One could talk it over with them, in a prophylactic way. He might be a crank or something. In that event he needs treatment . . . Shall we have a spot of shut-eye?"

I pushed off from the bank before it started to get really dark. The colonel was asleep, his head propped up on his hat. The dawn overtook me off White Cottages; the anchor kept me in place in the light early morning breeze.

The shoreline here is sloping and from the water the lakeside dachas stand out well. The industrious senior citizens were already stirring into life in their front gardens. In their pyjamas, old striped trousers, and threadbare service jackets, they were fiddling around their beehives with their smokers, or heaping up the earth around the foot of their apple trees, or hoeing along the rows.

The fish were gobbling up the bait on my hooks. I didn't look at the floats. White Cottages made me see red. Watching these people who had served out their time in the organs, I tried to guess which of them had been the first to floor Isaac Babel or Vsevolod Meyerhold with a blow of his fist.

I made an effort to understand what it was that they saw now, in the early morning, when they raised their sleep-filled eyes to the sky.

Do they really see that same sun?

Can there exist a guideline telling them to see the sun?

One person whom your Sasha Belyavsky could not have told you a thing about, Zinaida Borisovna, is my friend from the Leningrad siege, Yasha Gurin.

Before his death I had known him for three years – but that would be a silly way of looking at it in Yasha's case.

Each of us is bound to have one such friend, the memory of whom is enough to deter you from doing something bad. Where I am concerned, I am capable of stooping to anything, but skinny little Yasha even today keeps popping up before me with his red-hot, consumptive's eyes. I recall his slightly moist handshake. He kept scrubbing his hands into a ball and moaning: "The blighters have started sweating again."

He had a large, generous mouth with wide, bloodless lips.

I do not know the details of his biography. Once I used to indulge my curiosity, and by asking a person all about himself, I reckoned to form a judgement of him. But in due course I found that an individual's curriculum vitae did not serve as a guide to the peculiar features of his life. I saw for myself how a wide range of biographies was fed into history's pitiless grindstone and emerged as a shower of fine particles from which it was indeed difficult to discern nature's original design. So I started forming my judgement of someone the moment I first set eyes on him. It was important for me to understand what he had succeeded in preserving from his own shards. And whether they had been reassembled anew.

Of Yasha I knew only what I saw. In 1941, when I got to

know him, he bore a close resemblance to a Komsomol member of the twenties. It was not just a superficial resemblance. Not merely the sports vest he loved to wear. He favoured the vest because he had no one to look after him – it could go without washing for quite a while. He had managed to preserve through those terrible years a belief of such purity that it lit him up from inside like a pocket torch. Rather than shine it straight into people's eyes, he used it to show us where we should step so as to avoid tripping.

At times I had the impression that he was living above all the tumult. A grimace of revulsion would cross his face whenever something vile occurred near him.

Yasha Gurin was our boss. As a department head of the Radio Committee from even before the war, he stayed on in this capacity during the siege. They turned him down for service at the front: his lungs were eaten away by tuberculosis, and he was exempted from call-up.

I had got on the Radio Committee by pure chance. While a teacher at the SSF, I had out of boredom done two or three radio broadcasts, the contents of which I do not recall. Gurin thought he discerned in me a latent talent for writing humorous sketches about minor human failings.

The scripts I wrote were broadcast once a month on a Sunday over the city relay network.

On Sunday 22 June there was no broadcast. I decided that the culprit was my ancient radio dish – which had fallen silent – and phoned Gurin.

He said: "There's some sort of cock-up. Half an hour ago Moscow gave orders to stop broadcasting and keep the whole apparatus at the ready."

[151]

My Institute was evacuated a month later. I remained behind in Leningrad.

War did not arrive instantly: bombardment of the city started on 8 September.

The two and a half months before that first frontline night was the period that saw the crystallization in everyone of their courage or their cowardice. The process did not end there. The siege lasted so long that in some cases courageous people turned into cowards and some of the cowards started acquiring stamina.

Human psychology, stripped down to a state of ignominious nakedness by the ravages of starvation and artillery bombardment, is not necessarily always symptomatic. It would be too harsh to form one's judgement of someone simply from the attributes he happened to display under these unnatural conditions.

The average life expectancy is sixty to seventy years. Within such a period the sudden, horrific convulsion of the siege accounted for a single year. Why should that one year be regarded as the most typical for the purpose of composing someone's profile? The ignominy to which that person stooped was often part and parcel of him. But it could and did happen that someone else was reduced to this state of ignominy by his own total degeneration. He became loathsome. It was unbearable to look at him. Yet it was no longer him. And, in fact, the only lesson to be drawn is that it would be best not to spend the entire siege in such a person's company. He cannot be relied on when he is starving like a wild beast, with no prospect of relief. But how can such a state of affairs be mankind's normal lot?

[152]

That was not how I thought in the winter of 1941–42. I was quick to condemn people and people were quick to condemn me in terms of those pitiless laws established by the siege. The psychosis of the state of emergency stayed active in our veins for a long time. Living under those unthinkable conditions, united by the same bestial fate, we more often than not treated with contempt those who had never drunk from this well.

Yasha said to me: "We must strike at the enemy with whatever comes to hand. Your task is to write satirical stories about the Fascists. Three times a week Leningraders must be able to have a good laugh when they read them!"

I was assigned this impossible task by Gurin soon after the beginning of the war. I was given an editor to work with me. Nowadays he is a Leningrad University professor, but then he was simply Yura.

Yura was the first to listen to what I had put together. When I got to the end of my feuilleton I would raise my eyes and see my editor's look of boredom.

"Not funny," Yura would say.

He would advance to the door and pronounce: "When you've made it sound funny, give me a knock from the inside and I'll open up."

The lock clicked and the door was now secure.

Among the torments I suffered during the siege, this agony at having to write funny things reduced me to tears.

Reading through the tragic Sovinformburo news bulletins, listening to the endless wail of the air-raid sirens, I laid in to Hitler and Goebbels.

I made mincemeat of them; all that remained of them was a damp patch.

But their armies had already got to Srednyaya Rogatka and their artillery was shelling the city from Voronyaya Gora. The public loudspeakers were all permanently tuned in to the city broadcasting network. Inside those solidly frozen flats, in the mist, above the streets strewn with broken glass, the only sound audible was the tick of the network's metronome. That uncomplicated instrument, once in use to measure off the rhythm of melodies, was now marking out the rhythm of our immediate fate.

For the first few weeks of the war the people on the Radio Committee had no idea of how to fill the hours of broadcasting. There were bulletins from the front, the ticking of the metronome, then Tchaikovsky's familiar young swans swam onto the sound waves, and the Indian Guest* enumerated his by now totally inappropriate wares – these chilly operatic offerings lavished their fragile charms on an unquiet ether.

If the war was due to become the city's daily fare, it was not yet on the menu.

"The radio has to speak!" Yasha spluttered. "It has no right to be silent. People can't live just on bad news bulletins!"

"Comrade Gurin," Kovalyunets, the Party regional committee instructor, butted in. "I don't like your attitude."

"I'm not fond of it myself," assented Yasha.

"On what basis do you consider the bulletins bad? It's part of the process of luring the enemy on."

Yasha wiped his crumpled handkerchief across his palms.

* A character in the opera *Sadko* by Rimsky-Korsakov.

[154]

He gave a smile: "Frankly, Comrade Kovalyunets, life would be a great deal more pleasant if we hadn't lured him on right up to Pulkovo."

We had long grown sick of the "luring on" formula. The people who used it most were those who were shortly to abandon the city.

It was not that easy in our radio broadcasts to hit on a tone which more or less corresponded to the life of the people of Leningrad. At first nothing seemed suitable. The customary back slapping, stiff-upper-lip attitude was insultingly phoney. There was enough to depress one even without the radio. Yasha Gurin tried to ensure that the truth was uppermost in our broadcasts. It could not and maybe should not have been total. The truth of the siege was so overwhelming and so horrendous that even the Lord above would have tried partially to embellish it. Leningrad had not to be deprived of hope. The city had the right to admire its own courage.

I am not now exaggerating things. I may have been lucky: I was surrounded by staunch friends.

I was living not far from the Radio Committee and as long as its employees had not entirely gone into enforced seclusion, various of them used to pop in on me to relax after a twenty-four-hour spell of duty. They slept on the floor any old how, on top of their greatcoats, with an assortment of rags for their bedding.

By some happy coincidence, my telephone was still working. There were times when Yasha managed to get a call through to Moscow. That was where his wife lived: none of us knew her.

"Lyalya," he would shout into the phone. "Lyalya dear,

everything's fine . . . Absolute rubbish, Lyalya, we're OK . . ." And, before hanging up the receiver, he would look at us shyly and speak into it more softly: "Lyalya dear, I love you."

In 1944, when the blockade had already been broken, he was handed over to be a soldier – tubercular, exempt, untrained as he was.

It happened all of a sudden.

The Radio Committee orchestra had been giving a public concert in the main hall at the Philharmonic.

Yasha impressed on the musicians that all should be as in peacetime – and they came out onto the stage in white dress shirts, tails and black ties around their scraggy necks.

It was icy cold inside the auditorium.

The audience, nicely warm in their fur coats, fur jackets, greatcoats and high felt overshoes, oohed and aahed rapturously when the musicians appeared on the stage. They were given an ovation even before they settled down to their instruments.

The most fervent reception came from Yasha. His applause kept him warm for at least five minutes: he was the only person present in that vast auditorium who was without an overcoat. In his badly ironed suit, in a crumpled but clean white shirt, plus a tie, and in spit-enhanced patent-leather shoes, Yasha stood well to one side, next to the end box, and clapped for all he was worth.

Instructor Kovalyunets said to him in the interval: "You're wrong, Comrade Gurin, to put it all on such a personal plane. The people sitting in the box are people whom the entire city knows and respects. They see it as their duty to keep their coats on, so as not to distance themselves from the public. What's the point of your demonstration?"

Yasha looked at him with large, uncomprehending eyes: "But I asked the musicians to come in tails! . . . Out of respect for their achievement . . ." His teeth were chattering with the cold, red spots flecked his hollow cheeks. "Anyhow, what business is it of yours?"

A few days later, returning from his meal at the Radio Committee canteen, Yasha spotted a freshly posted notice on the bulletin board: "Gurin, L. Ya. is discharged as a result of staff reductions." He did not bother to ask the Radio Committee chairman for an explanation.

He went to the recruitment office and within twenty-four hours had been posted to the front as a political instructor.

The news of his death was some time in reaching us. He was already lying in the military morgue when tentative moves were afoot to secure his return. Under pressure, Yura, my editor, had been collecting signatures for a petition that called for Gurin's reinstatement on the Radio Committee.

Our Chairman said: "If there was anything missing in our heroic city, it just had to be this – collective petitions. In siege conditions such collective appeals are a crime punishable under military law." He handed the signed petition back to the editor. "Take it. You did not write this and I did not read it." Fumbling in the drawer of his desk, he sighed: "Yasha was a good lad."

It has taken many long years of effort in our country for a person describing historic events to which he was a witness to have the right to do so in his own name.

It was not the done thing to use the pronoun "I". One had to write "we". "I" was considered improper. One had to speak solely in the name of the people.

For many this was a relief, because it is easy to bury an individual's grief amid the not readily verifiable achievements of the people as a whole. Just as it is a simple matter to conceal one's own limitations and foolishness under cover of the indisputable intelligence and gifts of the people.

I am not chronicling historical events. Old men are wont to recall events of their own past. My own was such that I took no direct part in the creation of the history of my people. My actions were of no historical significance. They occurred against the background of what was taking place around me. Whether I was part of that background or stood out from it is of no consequence.

I first realized this after the war. The siege of Leningrad had acutely sharpened one's sense of community. Each person's fate ceased to be a purely personal matter. However trivial the task I was performing on the Radio Committee, I had the idea that "we" needed it.

The city's face could be seen through the prism of my own fate. We all were at one with our city – in despair and in hope.

Accustomed by the war and the siege to think in terms of a community of interests, of involvement, I assumed that this feeling would grow stronger when victory came. It had to do so – we dreamed so much that it would!

We had the impression of counting for something. The war had dispelled my past doubts. I was convinced that we were about to make a fresh start. Respect for the people's sacrifices demanded a new beginning.

[158]

I wanted to see personal responsibility for what was happening.

I wanted my opinion to count.

In August 1946 we were all assembled in the Smolny. It was the first time I had been there.

A strange feeling came over me when I found myself in a long, broad corridor leading to the enormous high doors that gave onto the assembly hall. I almost choked in a flood of literary reminiscence. For me the whole building was imprisoned in quotation marks. In those first few brief minutes before we learned why we had been summoned there, I was, as it were, submerged beneath the avalanche of all I had heard about the Smolny.

The oak doors swung open. I became part of the quotation. I have not yet succeeded even now in extracting myself.

A portly man of average height in a well-tailored loose-fitting suit, with a thin moustache on his round, tubby face, came out onto the rostrum. I had often seen portraits of him. Now, in the flesh, he had acquired a pair of legs: until then I had become used to seeing him from the waist upward. In higher intellectual circles they usually referred to him, though not to his face, as Andrey Alexandrovich. No surname was needed. When his waist-length reproduction hung on the walls of the city streets, he was Zhdanov. With legs added, he was Andrey Alexandrovich; minus legs, Zhdanov.

On this occasion we, in our numerous gathering, had the benefit of the entire him, live, in the flesh – Andrey Alexandrovich Zhdanov. It had the sound, not of Christian name plus patronymic plus surname, but of a title, of a rollcall.

He crossed the dais from extreme right to left, past the table at which sat the members of the praesidium, and arriving at the speaker's rostrum, from which Lenin in 1917 had proclaimed the Soviet regime, deposited on it a pile of books – they had white paper markers protruding from them. His face was sullen. Even enraged. And he did not so much place the books on the dais as somehow fling them down.

He delivered his speech without getting up onto the rostrum but pacing to and fro beside it. The steps he took were full of wrath, of chagrin. He spoke without any hesitancy, not bothering to consult any notes. At times he went swiftly over to the rostrum, tugged out one of the books, opened it at the place marked and disdainfully read out a verse of poetry. Then he would toss the book back onto the pile.

I listened to the speech without any excessive respect for Zhdanov or any particular prejudgement. I listened to him as one might listen to anyone. I wanted to understand what he was getting at. Both my experience as a teacher and the dry exactitude of my subject, mathematics, taught me to listen to the meaning of the words and not invest it with any spurious halo.

The subject was literature, of which I had a good knowledge, and which I loved. I knew Zoshchenko's short stories and Akhmatova's poems. The view Zhdanov took of them stunned me. It seemed so monstrous to me that I looked around at least a dozen times during the speech to try to determine what other people were thinking.

Their faces were impenetrable.

Something unreal was happening before my very eyes.

Several hundred well-educated people were making a superhuman effort to control themselves, an effort that had to be muscular rather than mental, for only by immobilizing their muscles could they avoid rising from their seats, bursting into moans and taking leave of their senses. I subsequently grew used to such meetings, but for me this was the first occasion of its kind. An invisible destructive process was at work inside me and around me. There was something cracking, breaking up and snapping off inside us: the remnants tried to re-form, like soldiers – the ranks had broken.

Despite it all, no fewer than six hundred intelligent people, many of whom bore undying personal respect for both Zoshchenko and Anna Akhmatova, six hundred persons who had gone through the horrors of the recent war, sat impassively in their seats in the hall and listened respectfully to this prematurely corpulent, moon-faced man with the dandified moustache, irritably pacing to and fro in front of us, delivering his repulsively coarse twaddle.

The confusion in the hall was so great that even those few speakers who hastened to the rostrum in Zhdanov's wake failed at such short notice to mobilize their reserves of hypocrisy: their brief speeches were pathetically inadequate, even in the cause of infamy.

I emerged from the Smolny at one o'clock in the morning.

On my way back in the suburban electric train I looked with envy at the other people filling up the compartment: they as yet knew nothing. And I was desperately sorry for them – they would have to learn about it tomorrow.

My fellow passengers were young boys and girls who would have to drum into their heads what I had just had to listen to.

They were babes in arms for whom it would come to seem quite natural.

They were old men who would have to carry it with them to the grave.

The following day and for many years to come this pronunciamento was to acquire the force of law.

From that night onward life for me lost all practical logic. The consequences of the Smolny meeting went beyond the fates of the two writers, Zoshchenko and Akhmatova. And it was not even literature's future that gave me cause for concern: in time it would find its proper place once more – that I could visualize, albeit with difficulty.

It was the speed and simplicity with which people adopted an alien, inane and vicious point of view as their own – that was what astounded me. The astonishing fervour that people, by now eagerly, put into propagating this point of view, into advertising it backwards and sideways, beating their comrades, both the living and the dead, over the head with it.

One has to have a very low opinion of mankind to imagine it readily assenting to commit acts of infamy. I have had a great deal of experience as a teacher and I always had the clear impression that the class or auditorium which I was about to instruct consisted of good people. Of people destined to perform decent acts. It had been programmed into them by nature. When I look at an adult, I habitually ask myself: What was he like as a child?

It seems to me that in the case of the best people their childhood is related to their adulthood like figures in a geometrical progression. Even in his mature years a good man can be seen to have something childish about him.

The fully developed, obtuse scoundrel raises discomfiting thoughts. Before he appeared on earth as he is now, nature had been working on him for millions of years. It lavished all the resources of its magical, gradualist art on the creation and perfection of this organism. It conducted him through thousands of metamorphoses: he was amoeba, fish, dolphin, monkey – nothing but the very best was good enough for nature's favourite, ultimate creation. The secret of the albumen from which he is formed is still unknown. The mysterious structure of his brain, the millions of superintelligent cells that go to make up his being, baffle the imagination. What do you have to do to yourself, what wickedness do you need to perpetrate on this entire organism to reduce kind, industrious nature's titanic efforts to nil? Why does he need it all? What's the use to him of this subtle arrangement of grey matter (which is the property of one and all) or this operative nervous system, with its lightning response, its speed of thought? For him, even a white shirt, a tie, or the act of shaving is superfluous. He might just as well go around covered in nothing but his fur, armed with a stone axe, and take up his abode in the forest, the taiga, the pampas or a cave, to become lord of the wild beasts – he is after all a troglodyte – rather than inflict his presence on mankind.

It's almost time, Zinaida Borisovna. As soon as I sort out my affairs, I'll come to see you in Samarkand. So what do my affairs amount to? Nothing, really, the dismal process of getting used to one's old age.

At times I have the impression that my writing is poisoning my system. The virus took root and now it is uppermost.

Do you know, Zinaida Borisovna, what night is like for an old man? Whatever I turn my mind to – there's no peace. As if I had the most sensitive of receivers grafted into my skull. It has a dual source of energy: connected to the network of my past, it operates on the worn-down batteries of my conscience. It has no unobtainable stations. Nor any jammer. By an effort of willpower I try to switch it from one wavelength to another. It is not the Voice of America – it is my own voice.

Sleep eludes me.

Let's try thinking of something different. Of fishing. There were some good bites in Latgalia in a little place called Zeineshke . . . My tackle was pretty lousy. Baited with shrimp. But congers like gudgeon. They really respond to gudgeon. Don't get sidetracked . . . Yes, they really respond to gudgeon. But then along came the postman with the newspapers. And they carried the news about the doctor-assassins. Time to switch away from that wavelength.

Where did we get to? The last time we stopped at logarithms. A logarithm is the index of the power by which the base needs to be raised to achieve a certain figure. Remember. 030103. 047712. The booklet giving Przhevalsky's Tables. This one is Gauss. And there's Neper. A whole lot of things. Secants. And cosecants too. They won't have any bother. Comrade Gauss, do you plead guilty? Guilty. Neper and I wanted to bring back capitalism in Soviet Russia.

Perhaps the silence is preventing me from getting to sleep. If only a cricket would chirrup. Where've they all gone to, those crickets? What's that – a grasshopper? Or are grasshoppers something different? I think grasshoppers are cicadas. I wonder how many generations of cicadas have gone by since that time in Batiliman?

I went to see Igor Astakhov in 1954. He was living in south-west Moscow in a new house. We had never been on familiar terms. But after the long absence I found myself using the familiar "thou" to him as if we were blood brothers. His new wife was with him in their new flat. I do not remember her face: she merely served at table and sat quietly in the background. It was not I who started talking of Katya. Igor did. Then he got to his feet and walked over to the sideboard on which there was a wooden box shaped like a small trunk. "Do you recognize it?" asked Igor. I recognized it when he opened the lid and removed the contents. She was wearing a Juliet-style skull cap the night I met her in Tashkent. A red cloth one, decorated with brilliant little circles . . . And with a little arrow in the middle. Something like an embroidered Central Asian tyubeteika. "That's not everything," said Igor. He pulled a blue, silk shift out of the trunk. I asked: "Didn't it get mixed up? Maybe they gave you someone else's? After all, they had a lot of women's underwear." "I don't think so," Igor replied. "In that respect they had everything in good order. Drink up. There's still more for you to know." I drank up. His wife fingered the side of the teapot and took it away to the kitchen to warm it up. She took a long time doing so: she was still warming it up when I left. "There are new people there now," Igor said. "Somewhat confused lads. The one who called me in kept rubbing his face with his hands as if he had gone and got it frozen. He suggested going for a stroll in the sunshine. We walked from the Lyubyanka to the little square

[165]

in front of the Bolshoi and sat down on a bench. 'You probably realize,' he said, 'that Ekaterina Fyodorovna has been rehabilitated. Believe me, I find it hard to tell you, but her rehabilitation is posthumous.' I asked the lad for how long she had been inside. He replied: 'Not long. A month and a half.' Then I asked him what she had died of. He replied: 'She committed suicide.' Of course," Igor said, "I asked him how it had happened. He said that the manner of death had not been recorded in the case papers. Then he extracted Katya's things from his briefcase and handed them to me. And the miniature trunk is not hers – it's mine: I simply put the things inside it."

That same dratted wavelength over my receiver. And more than adequate reception – nightly.

I'm unlikely to get to sleep now. Perhaps a spot of poetry. "On the cry: There's mutiny brewing, he would wrench free the gun at his waist" . . . Better something longer and a bit more restful . . . "He served the State with zeal and nobly; his father kept afloat on debt, would hold grand balls for all the gentry, and blue'd the lot, his debts unmet." Or . . . "Everything cloys in course of time, but thou my love shall never pall, tho' the days flit past and the years go by and the centuries slow to a crawl . . ."*

"You'll sign in any case, you bitch. Very well, lads, show this whore where to find the fifth corner of the room."

What was I doing at that moment? How did I dare do anything at such a time? Everyone did things and I did too.

* Extracts from poems by, respectively, Gumilyov, Pushkin and Pasternak.

Maybe at the very minute when she was searching for the fifth corner in a four-cornered room, I was somewhere laughing. Maybe I was sitting in the theatre. Maybe I was alive – at that moment?

"OK, you can cart her away now, so she can really think things over. You better do some thinking, you hear me? Stop all this nonsense. Your dad pegged out in prison and you'll be doing the same."

I telephoned Zinaida Borisovna from Dushanbe and gave her the number of my train and the carriage.

To tell the truth, I got very nervous thinking about the meeting. We had been exchanging letters over a period of five years or so. They had not been all that frequent and we had exhausted the subject matter in them. But Zinaida Borisovna's actual existence gave my past a jolt. It might have occurred irrespective of her – as a logical consequence of my being an old-age pensioner. However, the presence of someone who knows the details of your life provides you with a collocutor. I had someone to turn to.

In turning to her I tried forming a careful picture of her in my mind's eye. I could not have put it in words and I did not try. It was of no importance to me. My overheated imagination conjured up a figure that was close to me in spirit, something not made of flesh and blood. It was composed of particles of my own life and of other people's lives.

Zinaida Borisovna's letters provided little substance for the imagination. She never wrote about herself. She left my politely diffident questions unanswered. All I knew was that

[167]

she worked in the Foreign Languages Department of Samarkand University.

Now I remember – her letters did at times surprise me. But my surprise always registered retrospectively. At the time of receiving her letters, I was not surprised by them. When I read them, they did not prompt questions. Zinaida Borisovna was not important to me – Who was she? Where was she from? What sort of a person? – all this was immaterial. The important thing was to have a catalyst in Samarkand through whom the eerie ghosts of the past could make contact.

I arrived in Dushanbe by plane from Moscow and phoned her in Samarkand the same day.

Our conversation was brief.

Briefer than I had expected.

Maybe this was because I had got so accustomed to the tone used in our letters that I lost my head when I heard the unfamiliar voice. Maybe I was under the impression that the voice was bound to be familiar to me, but it was completely unfamiliar. A voice not carrying any associations. As I replaced the receiver, the thought occurred to me that Zinaida Borisovna was experiencing the same feeling.

When the slow Dushanbe train, half empty and dusty, drew into the station at Samarkand, there was no one waiting on the platform. I was standing in the connecting passageway behind the back of the attendant at the top of the carriage steps and at first failed to spot the woman walking slowly along the length of the train. I probably took her to be one of the station staff. She wore an extremely shabby, long black coat done up at the neck by the upper two buttons but left negligently open over her stomach, and a pair of large masculine brogues. She was now parallel to me.

My eyes had sought out Zinaida Borisovna, the lady who had promised to meet me – and I had seen no one.

I looked at her more carefully. She gave me a broad smile: her face was unprepossessing.

I do not know why, but I felt a strong wish that she should not turn out to be Zinaida Borisovna.

My recollection of Sasha Belyavsky was that of a slightly dandified, intellectually refined young man, and I found it impossible to connect him in my mind with this woman. Her smile made her even less attractive. Her trouble was not her age but her unkemptness. There was something unkempt not only about her clothes but about her face too. She wore an absurd silly little hat, too small for her large face, perched askew on top of her dishevelled hair. She had an ugly protuberant mouth – with teeth missing.

I spotted all this at once, cursing myself for my capacity to find fault.

We introduced ourselves at the entrance to the carriage.

Zinaida Borisovna had assumed that I would stay with her, but I begged off in favour of a hotel.

She took my refusal badly.

"I am expecting so much from our meeting," said Zinaida Borisovna. "After all, you were Sasha's best friend."

She escorted me to the hotel and waited while I registered. She was unable to stay longer – they had only given her an hour and a half off work.

"Do you have a lecture to give?" I asked.

She replied: "I don't have lectures to give. I'm a laboratory assistant in the department. You must come and see us at the University. Perhaps you can compare work experience."

I mumbled something back. Already at the station I had the impression that she was not really listening to what I said. "You haven't changed much," Zinaida Borisovna said. "Just as I imagined you from what Sasha said about you . . . So, this evening you'll come over to my place."

I spent the day tramping around Samarkand.

Indifferent to the appeal of ancient architecture, I roamed over the stone floors of venerable mosques, pausing for a moment to look at the burial vaults.

My reaction was one of cold admiration.

I was unable to appreciate the regal magnificence of these edifices. I am far from seeking to impose my viewpoint on anyone, but now that I found myself in Samarkand, I felt surfeited with the bloody history of mankind. Majesty achieved by such means was not to my liking. They chopped people's heads off, poisoned them, flogged them, stoned them – and then erected monuments to themselves of incredible beauty. I was fed up with such lords and masters even if they had unrivalled artistic taste.

I know I was supposed to admire the works of the unknown craftsmen, but even this did not work out genuinely. Behind all this beauty I perceived only an Asiatic talent for submission and servility. The sheer monotony of human cruelty, going back to the depths of the centuries, finished off my disenchantment here in Samarkand. Nothing had been newly contrived. It had all existed before.

In the evening I went to visit Zinaida Borisovna.

She lived on one of the streets that have undergone no

change in the last hundred years. Featureless, single-storey houses sloped down the side of a dusty, unsurfaced hill. They stood in close proximity to one another, separated only by solid wooden gates into which low openings had been let. Apart from the television aerials there was nothing to remind one of the second half of the twentieth century. And the aerials were not much help. If one is seeking to plot a route through the decades, *they* are not the thread that will help you to get your bearings on real life.

"I copied out Sasha's poems for you," said Zinaida Borisovna. "They're in this exercise book. And these are the photos of him. His letters to me are in the large envelope. Have a look while I set the table."

I sat down in an elderly velour armchair next to the Dutch oven. Zinaida Borisovna had headed toward the passageway where she had a Primus on the boil. But on the way there she suddenly flopped down onto the revolving chair beside the open piano and, fingering the keys, struck a chord.

"I tuned this instrument specially for your arrival," she said.

And left the room.

I started to examine what she had put down on a small table in front of me. It did not amount to all that much – considerably less than I might have expected.

Sasha's poems I was familiar with – they were all dated around the time we used to meet in Kharkov. And the half dozen photographs were from the same period – perhaps a shade later. I made no attempt to go through the small bundle of letters – when I partially undid it, I spotted four with the address written in Sasha's neat handwriting. The return address on them was in Kharkov. When I clumsily turned the

[171]

envelope over, a page of one of the letters fell out. It started: "Dear Nina, there's no point in your reproaching me . . ."

I read no further. Zinaida Borisovna had come into the room. She asked: "You're doubtless surprised that Sasha wrote to me so little?"

She looked hard at me.

"There is no reason for you not to read his letters. I make no secret of them."

We sat down to have a cup of tea. I felt increasingly uncomfortable and disappointed. But Zinaida Borisovna noticed nothing. Her manner was confident and assured. There was a kind of proprietary note in what she said about Sasha, as if she had a titular right to reminisce about him. I could not see it that way. The greater the detail she went into, the more emphatic became the impression she conveyed of intimacy with Sasha. His youthful perceptions and views of twenty years ago had been preserved inside her as if in a refrigerator: there they lay untouched and unexpended.

I asked: "Which year did you get to know him?"

"In '35. Sasha was doing his postgraduate course and I was on holiday in Feodosia. In fact, I lived in Feodosia. But he must have told you about that."

"We seldom saw one another," I said.

"He didn't like writing." She chuckled. "All his friends complained about it. Even little Olya Kolotilova."

"Who's she?" I asked.

"Good Lord!" said Zinaida Borisovna. "Don't you remember little Olya! She lived next door to you. On Sadovaya Street at the corner of Chernoglazovsky. Chernoglazovsky goes this way and that's Sadovaya. Your windows looked out onto

[172]

her gates. Wait a moment, I'll get her photo out for you."

The photograph showed Olya Kolotilova as a small, wizened old lady. I grasped that she was small: she stood in some tiny square, holding on to the back of a bench and barely showing above it. Pigeons were feeding at her feet.

"Recognize her?" asked Zinaida Borisovna.

"No," I said.

"What a strange person you are. Sasha remembered everyone."

I wanted to tell her that he had died a quarter of a century ago and that it was not certain who would have remained in his overtaxed memory had he lived till now – but I did not have the courage.

"Was it long ago that you saw Kolotilova for the last time?" I asked.

"Olya? I never once clapped eyes on her," said Zinaida Borisovna. "But that doesn't matter. We exchange letters regularly."

"How about in Kharkov?" I asked. "When you were living in Kharkov . . . ?"

"I never lived there," Zinaida Borisovna replied. "I told you a moment ago that I met Sasha in Feodosia."

She sounded distressed at my muddleheadedness.

But there was something that still escaped me. And this began to get on my nerves, although I realized perfectly well that my irritation was quite out of place.

Making an effort, I said: "Forgive me, Zinaida Borisovna. Unfortunately, my meetings with Sasha before the war were not that many. And perhaps you are exaggerating the closeness of our friendship. The war did keep us far apart."

She looked at me in astonishment.

"But one's youth is an eternal part of one."

"Would that it were so!" I said. "In my case it's been seriously contaminated."

"But it's the one thing I live for."

An unknown, elderly, unattractive woman was sitting with me in the room, over the teacups. Only now did I notice how unusual everything around us was. It was all adventitious, transported here from the past. A glance at her possessions sufficed to evoke their old designations – chiffonier, ottoman, wardrobe, upright piano – and when they acquired these names they were already outmoded. I do not like the furniture of today. I find it too ready made, lacking in personality, lifeless. But this room typified the other extreme: the possessions in it had lost their former owners; life had gradually drained out of them and they stood defunct, unrelated to one another.

"It's easier for you," I said. "You kept on seeing Sasha until he left for the war."

"No," said Zinaida Borisovna. "We didn't have a single meeting after Feodosia."

Realizing the extremity of my tactlessness, I asked: "And how long did it last?"

"Why do you say 'did it last'? It's still lasting now. I had no one other than Sasha. When he died, his friends became my close friends."

"Which of them have you seen?"

"Not one. You're the first."

I could not visualize her life. I asked: "How do you come to know so much about us all?"

"I wrote letters. I received answers. After all, you were one of those who replied. There were others too."

"But why," I asked, "why did you not come and visit Kharkov prior to the war?"

"The opportunity did not arise. Sasha was against it."

The amazing thing was that her voice betrayed not a hint of regret. She spoke triumphantly, as if that was precisely the path her relations with Sasha had had to take.

By all normal standards she was deserving of pity. Logically I understood this, but, readily compassionate as I am, I could find in myself not a scintilla of pity for her. I did not take to her. I was unable to visualize her as other than I saw her now. My reaction was unjust to the point of cruelty, but I was in a quandary. I simply could not admit her through the gates to my past.

"Don't imagine it was a mere seaside romance," said Zinaida Borisovna. "Sasha read me his poetry and we discussed all sorts of things. If the war had not happened it might all have turned out differently . . . Let me play you something we both loved."

Without waiting for my agreement, she heaved her massive body from the table to the piano stool.

"Come and sit over here," Zinaida Borisovna requested. "I need to see the expression on your face."

She started to sing, accompanying herself on the piano. I have no idea what she read from my face.

Her thick fingers hammered at the keys, the piano vibrated beneath her heavy hands. And above it came the sound of her laboured singing.

Then at the climax of my shame for her came the sudden

thought: There must be people who find me comic. Another thought occurred: Is it really so comic when someone you did not love starts collecting together everything that remained of you, twenty years after you abandoned her and long, long after you yourself ceased to be?

For the first time I looked at Zinaida Borisovna with compassion and admiration.

While she, mouth agape, exhausted with the effort, finally came to the end of her song.

"Open the gate, my dear."

And I opened up to her and let her through – to Sasha.

I have no pupils now. My teaching zeal is directed inwards. I am standing in front of myself. We are now the same age.

"How did you make out?" I ask.

"I got by," he answers.

"What do you mean by that meaningless expression?"

"That I survived."

"No more than that?"

"You know" – he becomes heated – "I'm pretty fed up with you."

"And I too. We're fed up with one another but there's no way out for us. After all I have the right to put my questions to someone."

"Go ahead. Let's have them."

"Let's start at the beginning. How did you make out?"

"On a hand-to-mouth basis."

"But I hope you didn't betray anyone in doing so?"

"Depends what you mean by it."

"We're getting nowhere. Let me have a straight answer: Did you or didn't you?"

"To be exact – I did."

"As far as I know, what you're thinking of is what's normally called complicity. You just avoided saying anything, wasn't that it?"

"Yes."

"But there were occasions on which you stayed silent while inwardly protesting, inwardly seething?"

"And how! Many, many times. With my heart turning over in my mouth."

"But why did you stay silent? From fear?"

"Not only. Mainly – but not only. I was bowled over by the uselessness of any protest. My protest would have changed nothing."

"It's a handy theory," I said.

"Go to hell," he said. "You know perfectly well that's how things were. People more important than I also stayed silent. And I don't think they did so simply out of fear for their own skin. A protest would have meant their coming to an immediate, inglorious end, whereas by continuing to live they had the possibility of being of use. They performed their individual tasks well and honestly."

I asked: "Do you agree with that point of view?"

He replied: "No."

"Then why do you put it forward?"

"Because I can't think up anything better. All the other lines of argument are more despicable still."

"Why think up anything? What happened, happened. Why

do you keep picking at it? Concentrate on a new start, right from the beginning."

"But I don't know where the beginning begins. And is there such a thing in history?"

"An interesting line of thought. You give the impression of someone poisoned by his own biography."

"One moment," he said. "It's my turn to ask the questions."

"Go ahead," I said.

One of us was reputed to be a prig and the other was doing his very best to make a good impression.

The prig asked querulously: "But you do believe in something, don't you?"

"Well, it's like this . . ."

"Don't duck the question! Let's have a straight answer from you. Just as if your life depended on it. Do you believe?"

"I believe but I can't put it into words."

"What a strange belief if you can't put it into words!"

"Well, one can, but once you start putting it into words it becomes not very convincing. Maybe it's best so. Mankind has had a surfeit of formulas; from the most monstrous to the most ennobling. And I've come to a conclusion that may seem to you a bitter one . . . I simply, straightforwardly believe in goodness."

"In what sense?" the prig inquired.

"In the sense that it will prevail."

"And do you intend to assemble your followers under that banner?"

"I have no intention of assembling followers! I keep telling you so! My faith is without a form of words. I have no banner. But if you insist on taking from me what I have, what remains despite everything, I should be a completely lost man. Without this faith I would be even more lost than I used to be."

"Mere words! I want to know what you've held on to, what you have."

"Everything I started with. I have nothing else, do you realize, nothing! I have been through everything the world offered, everything mankind dreamed up. None of it suits me except what I believed in at the very start. I know what you're about to say. You're going to say that your life was not in keeping with it. Maybe so. It ought to have been! Things happened which I cannot make sense of. I cannot get around. to thinking that what happened was predetermined. I have the small segment of ground on which I am standing. Please do not touch it."

"I'm not proposing to touch it," I said. "All the best!"

"Where are you off to?" I asked.

"I don't know. In fact, I've got nowhere to go."

More years went past. A century, two centuries. I forgot none of it. Human memory has the one fantastic property of forgetting only that which deserves to be forgotten.

As time passes, memories curl up at the corners like old snapshots but still live to flower again. Flower into detail . . .

I did not have a single photo of Katya. We had never exchanged photos for the other to keep – the passion for immortalizing oneself on celluloid had still not become universal. In our youth it was not often that people had photographs taken of themselves.

It was perhaps a good thing that I had not a single picture of her. It would then have been even more difficult for me to

[179]

imagine myself, my today's self, standing side by side with her. Without her portrait it becomes easier for me to see myself as a young man: the pair of us exist only in my imagination. We are peers. We did not grow old side by side. No effort of imagination is required on my part to see her in all her beauty. Time has not destroyed her.

She invested me with a magician's powers. I have only to wave a wand over my memory and there is Katya again coming to meet me – coming as often as I choose. In Kharkov, in Leningrad, in Batiliman – it makes no difference. She comes toward me across unknown territory, from the other side of the planet.

I cannot remember what she is wearing. I cannot remember a single dress of hers – I don't need the detail. Thunder, storm, rain or shine – or the whole lot together (I don't care a fig that that can't be). When I see her coming toward me I forget which century it all happened in. The only thing that matters is that she reach me.

I have forgotten the colour of her eyes and hair. I have not even retained in my memory a word portrait of her. If you were to describe her features to me I would not be able to identify them. She was to me an indivisible whole. Such that I was ready to run away from her to the world's edge. Such that I was ready to crawl after her to the world's edge.

My next-door neighbour, a former political officer in an infantry company and now a philosophy teacher in one of the Leningrad institutes, has for the last ten years in succession spent his holidays on hiking trips. With his rucksack on his back, in tough, heavy walking boots, he takes the train to

Velikie Luki and from there proceeds on foot along trails known only to him.

It was here, in this area, that his entire company met their death. My neighbour, who has a retentive memory for the place names of the battles, circles round and round, trying to track down his comrades' burial places. They have long since become overgrown with grass or weeds or standing crops, or their decaying bones are now part of the foundation of some cluster of agricultural buildings, but he persists in raking over the ground like a sapper armed with a mine detector. In those ten years he has not found all that many graves. But it has become his main purpose in life. After surviving autumn, winter and spring in the Institute he waits impatiently for the summer vacation to arrive, and then, donning his knapsack, his trusted footwear on his feet, he sallies forth, stick in hand but unarmed, back into the front line.

In the village soviets, the collective farm managements, the rural cottages of the rebuilt villages, they are well acquainted with the indefatigable hiker. At first they showed consideration: fenced in the burial places which he tracked down in uncultivated areas; put a cement border round the grave-stones, and planted a circle of larch cuttings around it. Local dignitaries pronounced important speeches, the local newspapers carried a report of it with a blurred photograph of the meeting – by all accepted standards, the question had been exhaustively explored and put to bed.

The ex-political officer, however, continued with his visits to the area the next year, and the summer after that, and gradually got on people's nerves. The force which had perished in this locality was a reserve company pulled back from somewhere in the Novgorod area; none of its soldiers had any relatives in the locality, and people had grown tired of grieving over unknown bones. And there was barely a handful of the old people left who had been eyewitnesses and had not been mown down by the war. No one remembered a thing, or could give you an idea of the battle fought to save the district.

The hiker still continues to poke around the area, wearing the life out of everyone with his questions and his demands – not to mention the fact that it's summertime, the height of the season. People are starting to think of him and speak of him as someone with a screw loose, not quite right in his mind. A chap so afflicted by the war that he can't come to his senses.

From our meetings in our courtyard, our talks in the gentle, light spring evenings in the back garden, I have realized that we are both suffering from the same form of dementia.

We are both wanderers among unlocated graves.